VICENARY

A Collection of Black and African Culture
Science Fiction and Fantasy Stories

George Allen Blacken

Apostolic Pentecostal Alliance Books LLC

BARBERTON, OHIO

Printed in the United States of America

Published by Apostolic Pentecostal Alliance Books LLC, Ohio
www.apabooksllc.com

The Apostolic Pentecostal Alliance Books LLC name, logo, and colophon are the trademarks of Apostolic Pentecostal Alliance Books LLC.

ISBN: 978-0-9989630-8-2 (Printed Edition)

ISBN: 978-0-9989630-9-9 (Electronic Book Edition)

Library of Congress Control Number: 2020921538

Publisher's Cataloging-in-Publication Data

Names: Blacken, George Allen, author.
Title: Vicenary : a collection of black and African culture science fiction and fantasy stories / George Allen Blacken.
Description: Barberton, OH : Apostolic Pentecostal Alliance Books, 2020.
Identifiers: LCCN 2020921538 (print) | ISBN 978-0-9989630-8-2 (paperback) | ISBN 978-0-9989630-9-9 (ebook)
Subjects: LCSH: Short stories. | Fantasy fiction. | Science fiction. | African Americans--Fiction. | American fiction--African American authors. | Literature--Black authors. | BISAC: FICTION / Short Stories (single author) | FICTION / Fantasy / Collections & Anthologies. | FICTION / Science Fiction / Collections & Anthologies. | FICTION / African American / General. | GSAFD: short stories. | Fantasy fiction. | Science fiction.
Classification: LCC PS3602.L33 V53 2020 (print) | LCC PS3602.L33 (ebook) | DDC 813/.6--dc23.

Publisher's Note: This is a work of fiction. Names, characters, places, and incidents are a product of the author's imagination. Locales and public names are sometimes used for atmospheric purposes. Any resemblance to actual people, living or dead, or to businesses, companies, events, institutions, or locales is completely coincidental.

I thank my Lord and Savior Jesus Christ for providing the inspiration and making this book possible! This book is also dedicated to my wife of over fourteen years, mother, brother, children, and all others who have been there for me. I am grateful for all of the trailblazers who paved the way for me and future science fiction and fantasy authors.

CONTENTS

GRIOT

In the Variances of the Cosmos, there are infinite possibilities. One decision can change everything. The actions of a single person truly make a difference. Everything is connected, but yet retains what makes each component, system, universe, entity, and law unique.

I am Griot. I am able to cross through the barriers that separate the Variances of the Cosmos. I can see much, but have even more to learn. I have been a witness of many things, but not chosen to change the outcome of anything. My calling is to tell you what has happened so that you can make an informed decision on what comes next for you.

I am your storyteller sharing just a fraction of what the Variances of the Cosmos has to offer you. Also, consider me your narrator bridging the gap between worlds, and letting you know what makes someone tick. Everyone is on the clock. We must all make the most of whatever time we have left.

The time you spend listening to my stories and touring the Variances of the Cosmos with me will be well spent. Now is the time to relax and become refreshed. Leave behind the old reality and enter new worlds with unthresholded potential. Learn more about others and yourself through this journey. There will be both beginnings and endings. I will be with you every step of the way.

THE TOUR

"All systems are good! I am taking him out for a spin," Caliber said.

"Wait a minute, Caliber! This prototype from the African Union and the Eastern Empire alliance has not started trials yet," one concerned technician said.

"Consider this its first trial. It has done enough testing. Take it up with my father," Caliber said.

"Hey!" the technician said.

It was too late. Caliber and the prototype AA-4 already lifted off. Also, no one challenges Caliber's father, who runs the place. The technician just shook his head and reported this incident to his superior, who also shook his head.

Under Caliber's control, AA-4 speeds through the skies of Lagos, Nigeria with ease, dodging planes, helicopters, birds, and whatever else is in his way. "Who needs more contractor and school testing?" Caliber thought. Soon after, the authorities piloting enforcement robots come after Caliber and AA-4.

"Young man, stop what you are doing and return with us immediately!" the police officer said.

"I am conducting an official trial for the Rise Corporation," Caliber responded.

"Sure, you are. Now turn around!" the police officer said. As the enforcement robots closed in, AA-4 launched into a much higher altitude almost instantly.

"What the?" Caliber said.

The controls for AA-4 were no longer responsive as the console screen went out. "Work, you stupid controls!" Caliber shouted. AA-4 spun out of control and landed in the river near the bridge. Several enforcement robots released their aerial cranes to retrieve AA-4 and Caliber.

Like a bursting geyser, AA-4 jumps out of the river and right through the bridge with vehicles and pedestrians on it. AA-4 speeds right through the city streets plowing through and crushing whatever is in his way. As hard as he tries, Caliber cannot regain control of AA-4.

Then, the console screen comes back on, but the distorted screen points to signs of malfunction. AA-4's corrupted radar eyes mistakenly analyze all buildings as threats. No manual overrides work as AA-4 goes into an automatic offensive mode. AA-4's hands become flame throwers and incinerate downtown Lagos, Nigeria until a forced networked software upgrade sent from the Rise Corporation finally gets AA-4 to reboot and stand still.

Caliber exits out of AA-4. Then, AA-4 scoops Caliber up by his right hand and raises him up to a building to see downtown Lagos, Nigeria on fire. "No!" Caliber shouted. "I should have waited until the trials were done. I have dishonored my father," said a repentant Caliber. The authorities circled around Caliber. "I surrender," Caliber said. Caliber's father was fired by the board of the Rise Corporation that same night. No one has heard from Caliber and his family until this very day. AA-4 was further upgraded after failing its initial trials. Downtown Lagos, Nigeria had to be rebuilt and even stricter robot testing policies and procedures were developed and enforced. Many people died that night and several of the impacted families have yet to successfully rebuild their lives.

"Welcome to Jaya Science, Technology, Engineering, and Mathematics (S.T.E.M.) Junior High School," Principal Parman said. This presentation definitely got the Jude twins' attention. "Remember, that each of you in this group are chosen to be robot testers to prevent disasters like this or worse from happening. Let's continue the tour," Principal Parman said.

"Bolu, hopefully we do not screw things up like Caliber. This school never recovered after that," Chid Jude whispered to his brother, as they were exiting the auditorium.

"Don't worry, Chid, we are going to do just fine here," Bolu Jude said.

"I hope so, Bolu," Chid responded. Putting this hope in question was a pair of following eyes in the shadows watching the Jude twins.

There are the standard school things and then there are robotics. The Robotics Revolution transformed and united the entire continent of Africa, making Lagos, Nigeria the capital of the entire continent. Nigeria's top exports are robots, vehicles, and computer software. All three are developed and tested here at Jaya S.T.E.M. Junior High School, even though its limited budget often leaves its vehicles department neglected.

The simulation zones wake up the Jude twins in the tour. They are not the only ones fully awake. They walk into one of the constructive simulation zones that would remind the average onlooker of a computer lab, high tech arcade, and a fleet of console kiosks combined into something magnificent that is both entertaining and educational. This particular area is like a dream come true for the Jude twins, not realizing the nightmare cohabitating with them. The same following eyes from the auditorium appear on one of the kiosk screens with a frown.

Next on the tour, is one of the virtual simulation zones. Everyone in pairs is given a chance to try out a basic human-in-the-loop robot simulator. When the Jude twins finally get a chance to try out the robot simulator, the demoed program is suddenly overridden by a mysterious source. What served as a teaching tool has become a rollercoaster. The vibrations, rotations, and simulated drops make the world feel very small at an accelerated pace. As their world turns, the Jude twins dismiss a pair of staring eyes on the console screen as a hallucination. Chid is screaming like crazy while the adventurous Bolu laughs at the face of apparent danger. When they are about to black out, the simulator stops and they are freed.

"Are you boys alright?" one of the instructors said.

"We are fine," Bolu said. Chid is still dizzy as Bolu helps him get around.

"Did you see it?" Chid asked.

"I did, but it can't be," Bolu said.

"Youngsters welcome to Jaya," another instructor said.

"Thanks," Chid responded.

In one of the live simulation zones, they witness two robots engaging in a limited one on one fighting duel. No weapons are allowed in this particular duel. The bigger blue robot appears to have the advantage over the smaller red robot. The smaller red robot is able to avoid all of the blue robot's punches and grabs. Eventually, the red robot finds that one weak spot on the blue robot and knocks him out. As the blue robot falls, he launches his blue fist out of his right arm, which crashes through the window the Jude twins are watching the simulated duel. The launched fist barely misses the Jude twins. Everyone is baffled why such a malfunction happened. The watching eyes stare through the fallen blue robot eyes which ominously glow.

At the end of the tour, the Jude twins and students are shown the recently retired AA-4. This day, everyone in this tour becomes witnesses of the dead being resurrected. AA-4 wakes up from retirement and starts rampaging through the robot hangar. The students and staff scatter.

In spite of this scene being very chaotic, it appears that AA-4 knows exactly who his intended targets are. AA-4 walks towards the Jude twins, coming closer and closer. By the time the Jude twins reach the hangar exit, another malfunction slams the doors shut. AA-4 is getting closer and closer.

Right when AA-4 comes to grab the Jude twins, another robot operated by one of the instructors knocks AA-4 out. The hangar doors reopen and the Jude twins are out of there.

"Bolu, let's stop here," Chid said.

"A bathroom break is not a bad idea," Bolu said.

As Bolu is finishing up in a stall, Chid looks at a mirror. In the mirror, Chid sees someone other than himself. What he sees is a ghost that looks anything but human. While in his initial stage of shock, the ghost says something to him.

"I know your secret," the ghost said.

"Aargh!" Chid screamed.

"Chid!" Bolu said. He rushed out of the stall.

"Did you see that?" Chid asked.

"See what?" Bolu said. Something then tapped Bolu on the shoulder.

"Me," the ghost said. The Jude twins take flight. Then, they are dragged back. "You two are going nowhere," the ghost said.

"Who are you?" Bolu asked.

"I am Iparun, servant of Dideoluwa," the ghost said.

"What do you want with us?" Chid said.

"To have some fun off of you," Iparun said.

"What kind of fun?" Chid said.

"I can sniff you Christians out anywhere. Don't worry, I am not going to kill you yet," Iparun said.

"What?" Bolu said.

"I am going to have my fun with you first. It is going to be a long school year. Who knows? You might actually survive," Iparun said. Iparun then keeps laughing as the Jude twins exit the bathroom. Maybe a bathroom break was not such a good idea after all.

The Jude twins are also scolded for not returning with the group earlier. This is mild compared to what they faced earlier. Because of the confusion in the robot hangar, all of the students are sent home earlier.

As they ride the subway, the Jude twins make eye contact with each other but do not say a word. They know what each other are thinking. It is not safe to talk. They cannot share everything that happened this day with their friend and guardian, Uncle Jaiy. A diversity of people and things are welcomed in Lagos, Nigeria, but Christians are not on that welcome list. Uncle Jaiy is not too fond of Christians either. A lot has changed since the seven warlords conquered the seven continents of the world. There is much more to tell for this story at a later time.

CATECHISM

In some forests, there are towns, treasures, and other secrets waiting to be discovered. There is a hidden peninsula surrounded by water on three sides having many forests and its share of towns, treasures, and secrets. Danger, supernatural forces, and abnormal rogues have also taken residence here. Remember this hidden peninsula as Mesial.

Several hairy men that have forsaken their humanity come rummaging through an abandoned church in the forest once known as Providence. They have not come alone. They bring an unwilling female sacrifice with them, who is still resisting her forced calling.

When all hope appears to be lost, salvation then comes. A masked man in a black, red, and white bishop cassock robe wearing a red zucchetto hat emerges from the darkness hooking one of the hairy men by the neck with a golden crozier and stabbing him in the back with a silver dagger. Two other hairy men come charging at the masked man, but then just instantly collapse. The remaining hairy man grabs the golden cross and chain hanging around the masked man's neck. The masked man pulls off the glove of his right hand and lays it on the hairy man's face. The hairy man's face starts to burn. The hairy man screams in agony as what is left of his mind is also shut down.

The masked man then approaches the female previously set aside as a sacrifice. "Stay away from me Dark Bishop! I do not want to burn!" the woman yelled.

"It is okay," Dark Bishop said. He calms her down with his telepathy and uses his dagger to cut her loose.

"You are free," Dark Bishop said.

The woman quickly flees without even a thank you. It is true that whoever is convicted and does not repent is burned by Dark Bishop's touch.

Dark Bishop then uses what some call the fourth sight to both see and hear from the spiritual realm and other universes. A spirit in the shape of a bull responds.

"You have interrupted our preparations for the red moon sacrifice. We are coming after you tonight, no matter where you hide," the bull spirit said.

"I will be waiting right here," Dark Bishop responded.

"Then you will die where you were born," the bull spirit said.

"I was born to stop those like you," Dark Bishop said. It is true that Dark Bishop's origin started in Providence Church.

Let us go back fifteen years ago to a young minister, who was very active at Providence Church, where his father was the senior pastor and mother the first lady. Back in those days, Providence Church appeared to be on fire for the Lord. Unfortunately, that was not the only fire rising.

One of the older female missionaries was in tears about her missing husband. A young twenty-year-old minister promised to get to the bottom of this mystery. After one church service, when the young minister followed up with the older missionary, she had no recollection of the minister or what happened to her husband. She told the young minister to forget about such a foolish pursuit. Her husband ran off with a younger woman. The young minister told his father, who noticed other strange things happening in the church. The senior pastor started to ask the board and other members prying questions and preach more controversial sermons.

One night, everything forever changed during a Wednesday night bible study. The senior pastor and his family arrived for the bible study but noticed that no one else was in the sanctuary, even though there were multiple vehicles parked in front of Providence Church. Then, the five members of the trustee board came from two of the side doors with stoic looks on their faces.

"Reverend, we need to see you downstairs," the trustee board president said.

"Sure," the senior pastor said, as he motioned the first lady and young minister to leave.

"Let's go," the trustee board president said. The senior pastor was walking down the stairs to the basement, an area that was normally forbidden to everyone except the trustee board.

As the young minister and his mother left the church building, two men with bull masks appeared. Before a word could be uttered, the young minister and his mother were both struck down and dragged back into the church.

The young minister wakes up to find himself and his parents in handcuffs surrounded by a group with bull masks in the church basement. Even the trustee board members now had on bull masks. Some of the other participants also sounded like familiar congregational members.

Then, the senior pastor breaks the silence.

"You will not get away with this! Let us go!" the senior pastor said.

"Reverend, all you had to do was preach the word and inspire the people to give money. You were the perfect fool for our front. Now, we must find someone else to take your place," the trustee board chairman said.

"At least, let my wife and son go!" the senior pastor pleaded.

"There are no deals. You are more troublesome than Deacon Marshal," the trustee board chairman said. Deacon Marshal was the older missionary's missing husband.

"Prepare for your purging reverend," the trustee board chairman said.

The senior pastor is taken to what is called the thermal room. He is burned alive as a sacrifice to some form of bull spirit.

"Murderers!" the first lady said.

"No!" the young minister said.

Then, a woman with a bull mask walked up to the first lady and removed her mask. It was Missionary Marshal! During this brief moment of shock came another shock. Missionary Marshal stabbed the first lady in the chest.

"Throw her in the thermal room for more kindling," the trustee board chairman said. He then looked at the young minister. "Son, prepare for your catechism," the trustee board chairman said.

The young minister spits on the trustee board chairman's mask. The young minister is then punched in the chest by another member of this cult.

"Take our candidate to the memory room!" the trustee board chairman said. As the young minister is carried away, he hears how the memory room transformed Missionary Marshal.

In the memory room, the young minister is tied to an altar. "Son, tonight you become a vessel for God," the trustee board chairman said.

"God shall deliver me!" the young minister said.

"Tonight, you will see a real god at work!" the trustee board chairman said.

The ceremony begins with words in an unknown language being spoken. Then, a spirit with a bull head enters in the room.

"You shall be the next vessel for one of my children," the bull spirit said. He spits out a butterfly that flies into the young minister's mouth. "Embrace your transformation!" the bull spirit said.

The young minister is choking while moving uncontrollably. The young minister starts speaking in an unknown language that is not familiar to the participants. Then, comes a bright light. The young minister then vomits the butterfly, which is then consumed by fire. He starts to hear the fearful thoughts in everyone's minds. As a member of the cult comes to stab the young minister, he grabs his attacker by the hand and burns it. In his panic, the attacker's fire spreads across his body. The young minister screams out in rage and fear. The majority of the cult members that night experience a headache unlike any other and hemorrhage before they perish in their judgment. None of the trustee board is spared.

A man in white unties the young minister. "Let's get out of here now!" the man in white said.

"You will die fools!" the bull spirit said.

"Be gone, foul spirit!" the man in white said. The bull spirit cannot resist and departs. The young minister and the man in white depart the church just in time. A man on fire comes across something hooked up to the thermal room and Providence church goes up in flames.

"Young man, God did deliver you. Use your telepathy, fire touch, and fourth sight abilities well to spread the truth and administer justice," the man in white said.

"I will," the young minister said.

"Come follow me to Old Benny's Store. We have much to discuss," the man in white said.

"Yes," the young minister said.

When they arrived in Old Benny's Store, the rug in the back room led to an underground tunnel pointing the way to an alley in another town. This began the young minister's ten years in hiding, training, and true spiritual catechism. This young minister took on the mantle of the Dark Bishop to avenge the wrongs done by Providence Church and administer justice where ever else he is led to in Mesial. Dark Bishop also made it his business to enlighten the uninformed. It also became common knowledge for Providence Church to never be renovated or used again. When Dark Bishop emerged from his training and exile, finding Providence Church rebuilt, he shut it down once again.

Now, on the night of the red moon, things come full circle once again. The night becomes chilly.

"I am Stalactite, Bel's chosen champion this night. You will be sacrificed this night unto him," Stalactite said.

"What happened? Is Bel too afraid to face me?" Dark Bishop said.

"Die, infidel!" Stalactite said, as he launches several ice missiles from his hands toward Dark Bishop's way in rapid succession. Stalactite's mental barriers block out Dark Bishop's telepathy and he cannot get close enough to apply the fire touch.

Dark Bishop throws the golden crozier like a bo staff at Stalactite's boastful mouth. Some teeth are liberated and blood stains his icy figure. Stalactite bellows out in a fiery rage with chilling results. Chilly winds not previously known manifest along with a blizzard. It is becoming nearly impossible to breathe and Dark Bishop did not make it in time to apply the fire touch on Stalactite.

Growing in arrogance, Stalactite walks toward Dark Bishop, who is gasping for air.

"You cannot defeat Bel. You never had a chance," Stalactite said. In one of his few remaining breaths, Dark Bishop uses his fourth sight to see Bel chuckling. With his last bit of strength, Dark Bishop throws his anointed silver dagger at Bel's face he sees in the spiritual realm. This dagger crosses realms and hurts Bel. When Bel feels pain, so does Stalactite. This provides the Dark Bishop the opening he needs to apply the fire touch, which even penetrates Stalactite's icy form. The burning Stalactite pushes Dark Bishop away and flees.

Dark Bishop then hurries into the abandoned Providence church to find a populated basement with another red moon sacrifice in motion. Dark Bishop's telepathy puts a quick end to this secret ceremony since the distraction of Stalactite has been removed.

"Tonight, this ends!" Dark Bishop said to himself. He then takes some gasoline and burns down the remains of Providence Church the old-fashioned way.

Dark Bishop won this battle, but the war with Bel and his forces continues. Unfortunately, this is not the only foe in Dark Bishop's growing rogues' gallery. There are many more stories to tell of Dark

Bishop in Mesial. I cannot dwell in Mesial too long because Dark Bishop will eventually notice me with his fourth sight. We can't have that.

BDK

THE WORLD

"We have been in darkness long enough!" Stargel said to herself. The Torchbearers trained and appointed her as the chosen one to retrieve the eternal flame and return the light to the land. Even though she is human, she is different from the rest. The rest look human, but their minds have devolved into savage beasts. The Torchbearers told Stargel that the unique mixture and balance of light and darkness in her skin, blood, and soul made her immune to the syndrome that afflicted the rest of mankind.

Now is Stargel's chance to finally shine. She is twelve years old and has been preparing for this moment of her life. She is approaching the savage humans' camp where the eternal flame is hidden. The humans use the eternal flame to worship their god. This day, the false worship shall end and the power shall return to the people who need it the most. Stargel has been trained to not only fight, but outthink her enemy and use whatever situation she is in to her advantage.

The enemy camp is no more than a series of caves. The humans are living like rats running around in a maze they never seem to quite figure out. There is a passage leading to the mountain. On the mountain top is where the eternal flame is rumored to be.

To avoid being seen temporarily, the Torchbearers gave Stargel some invisi-gel, which gets into the body through digesting special gummy vitamins. With a limited supply of these invisi-gel vitamins,

Stargel must be very strategic when and how she uses them. She digests two of the vitamins, and it is as if she never existed.

Outside of the caves, there are people cooking, washing, playing, eating, drinking, and joking. When someone does not know better, it is easy to be satisfied in conditions as mediocre as this.

While heading to the caves, some dogs smell Stargel and they start barking and chasing after what they smell. While running from the dogs, Stargel runs into a hornet's nest. The hornets take care of her pursuers from there. The humans nearby also scatter. There is enough confusion aiding Stargel getting inside the caves.

The bats are the first to greet her in the cave. Her invisi-gel vitamins have worn off. Stargel will have to use the darkness to her advantage.

How will she find the eternal flame in this maze of darkness? She was told to follow the light, but sees no trace of the light within. Then, she sees the fireflies.

A group of them are traveling together in the same direction and Stargel decides to follow them. The fireflies leave the other humans in the cave in a trance. Stargel continues to follow the fireflies.

The fireflies lead Stargel to a spider web serving as a bridge over the chasm below. Stargel finds herself walking on a flimsy spider web. A giant brown and yellow spider with red eyes drops down coming closer to his dinner, Stargel. This causes the flimsy web to further shake, but Stargel maintains her balance. As the giant spider approaches Stargel, the group of fireflies stop what they are doing and just watch.

Before she can take another invisi-gel vitamin, the spider shoots some webs and pulls Stargel to him. She notices a river at the bottom of the chasm below and starts cutting through the web with a dagger to take a leap of faith into the river. Before she can take that leap, she is hanging on the bottom of the web bridge by a thread, with the spider's web previously used to pull her in, unwittingly helping her to do such.

As the spider comes nearer, Stargel takes another invisi-gel vita-min. The giant spider shakes the web bridge in frustration for a while, looking for his prey. Eventually, he spues out his webbing and goes about his business. As Stargel climbs up, the fireflies are waiting for her.

The fireflies next lead her to an overhead ledge she needs to climb to move forward. To Stargel, this is just like monkey bars. It is a good thing she sees it that way because if she falls, a pit of ravenous rats waits below. To further complicate matters, there are mice and roach-es she has to contend with while climbing over. Still, the group of fireflies just watch her, not proceeding without her.

As Stargel ascends, the forces of darkness put up a greater re-sistance. Stargel finds herself having to tiptoe through a pit of sleeping vipers. Each time one awakes, she has to stand still, even when they crawl all over her. Eventually, Stargel gets an opening and continues to move forward. The same group of fireflies waits for her.

Stargel goes into an upper room in the cavern and every time she exits this room, she finds herself back in the same room again and again. This time, the group of fireflies does not wait for her. They start to ascend. Stargel looks upward and they are at the top of a circular shaft.

Stargel walks around the room and starts to reach for things not seen as if they are seen. Eventually, Stargel feels something like a rope. She clings to the rope and starts to climb out of the room and into the shaft.

The shaft starts to spin as Stargel hangs onto the rope. The shaft starts spinning faster and faster. Whatever the rope is attached to also ends up rotating with the shaft. The shaft keeps rotating faster and faster. When all hope is lost, Stargel sees the light again.

Out of this light, something sticky and soft emerges. Stargel grabs it with one hand. This sticky and soft surface retracts, taking Stargel with it and out of the shaft. The light at the end of the tunnel is not what Stargel is thinking.

Stargel ended up catching onto a giant red frog's tongue that is about to swallow her. Sacrificing her dagger, Stargel barely manages to cut her hand free from the frog's tongue and hop away, while the fireflies watch from afar. This is time for another invisi-gel vitamin.

This is good timing because a mountain lion is waiting for her in ambush. Stargel keeps sprinting up the mountain path. Everything appears to be on track until she goes into darkness again.

There is a sleeping bear in the cave. Stargel is trying not to disturb the bear, walking with discretion. Unfortunately, the group of fireflies does her a disservice. Their light disturbs the bear. Then, they conveniently disappear.

As the bear wakes up, the forgotten mountain lion charges into the cave, looking for his mysterious prey. The lion and the bear have their showdown for dominance. Even though the fireflies did disturb the bear, that burst of light did show Stargel the way to proceed. She gets back on the straight and narrow out of the cave, to the mountain top.

The group of flying fireflies are there waiting for her, along with a glowing bushel on the ground. Stargel then hears a soft voice.

"Welcome child," the mysterious voice said.

"Who is speaking?" Stargel asked.

"Me," the mysterious voice said. The fireflies combine taking the shape of a golden midget with pointy ears.

"Who are you?" Stargel said.

"Who sent you?" the golden midget said.

"The Torchbearers," Stargel said.

"So, you think you are the chosen one?" the golden midget said.

"Yes, I have lived my whole life for this moment," Stargel said.

"Then, you had better be prepared, child," the golden midget said. "Only those who are worthy can use the eternal flame. Those who are not worthy, are consumed when touching the eternal flame. Are you willing to take such a chance, child?" the golden midget said.

"Yes. This is the only way that light can be restored to the land,"Stargel said.

"Then, let me ask this question, child," the golden midget said.

"Okay," Stargel said.

"Are humans worth saving?" the golden midget asked.

"No," Stargel said.

"Then, who are you doing this for?" the golden midget said.

"The Torchbearers," Stargel said.

"Do you pledge yourself to whom the Torchbearers serve?" the golden midget said.

"Yes," Stargel said.

The smile of a goblin as wide as a jack-o'-lantern emerges on the golden midget's face. "Remove the bushel and claim your prize, child," the golden midget said.

"Thank you," Stargel said. At her core, Stargel is a beautiful, kind-hearted child with only the best intentions in her heart.

As Stargel walks closer to the bushel, the golden midget's smile widens. The light underneath the bushel shines brighter and brighter. Stargel kneels down, about to remove the bushel covering the eternal flame. Then, it disappears.

"No!" the golden midget said. He then disappears too.

Then, everything else around Stargel disappears.

"Where are you? Where is the eternal flame?" Stargel said. She notices that she is now inside some kind of dome instead of being on the mountain top. "Release me!" Stargel said.

"Stargel, is not your name," an unknown black male said.

Stargel backs up. The black stranger walks closer to her.

"We can finally go home," the unknown black male said.

"Stay away from me!" Stargel said.

"That is no way to talk to your father," an unknown European female said.

"I have no father! The Torchbearers raised me!" Stargel said.

"I am your mother. You must come with us! There is not much time!" the unknown European female said.

Before Stargel can respond, she starts vomiting. Then, dizziness comes upon her and she blanks out. Stargel's real parents are able to liberate their daughter from captivity that day, making it back to their resistance's secret headquarters. Many sacrificed their lives that day for this mission to be successful.

Stargel has not been free since two years old. She spent the last ten years of her life a prisoner of the Star Empire, living in a virtual world being both brainwashed and indoctrinated by them. If Stargel would have uncovered the bushel and touched the eternal flame in this virtual world, her brainwashing would have been completed, made unbreakable and under the complete control of the Star Empire. Stargel came very close to losing it all, but was delivered from the darkness, coming into the light just in time.

Stargel's real name is Brittany Donica King. Brittany comes from her mother's grandmother meaning beautiful; kind-hearted, from Britain. Donica comes from her father's mother, meaning lady. King is the family name resulting from the marriage between her parents. Those who prophesied of this child's coming call her BDK. Many foretold a boy, not a girl, but she is BDK.

The prophecy states BDK growing up to form the Evangel Corps to oppose the alien ghosts known as the Star Empire. The Evangel Corps will use special weapons that can hurt the alien ghosts and free people from their possession. They will also carry shields that can capture these alien ghosts. They will free Earth from the Star Empire.

These alien ghosts have already secretly possessed many of the world's leaders and other influential people. It is a terrible thing for someone to be in bondage and not even realize such. There are more stories to share on the Evangel Corps.

ZONE RAIDERS

THE AMBASSADOR

Earth is now known as the barren Neutral Zone whose few remaining resources are controlled by a handful of sinister corporations who pay the citizens low wages with no benefits, treating them only a little better than slaves. Before Earth was made barren, many of its inhabitants left to form space colonies, which became zones. A zone is comprised of one or more space colonies. Warps were created to enable travel between zones. Presently, there are seven zones known to be inhabitable. Not counting Neutral Zone, which is also called Zone 0, the seven zones are: 1) Zone 1: Ice Zone, 2) Zone 2: Jungle Zone, 3) Zone 3: Desert Zone, 4) Zone 4: Fire Zone, 5) Zone 5: Water Zone, 6) Zone 6: Surreal Zone, and 7) Zone 7: Metro Zone.

All zones are at war with each other. The Universal Council, which once brought peace to the space colonies, disbanded publicly when the zones started to war among themselves. Because of the war, travel between warps is forbidden. The zones are constantly sending large monstrous constructs called Ambassadors through the warps to attack other zone space colonies. Battles in space itself are waged through ship and robot squadrons, but battles on the space colonies themselves are fought through sending Ambassadors and defending against visiting Ambassadors.

There are also refugees from Neutral Zone escaping to the zones from either the hidden warps or warps heavily guarded by automatons made by the large corporations to keep their cheap work force from leaving. There is an underground movement called One who have been smuggling people from Neutral Zone into other zones. One also sought to unite the seven zones and provide a more efficient means to fight the Ambassadors through seven Guardian teams of unity robots. Unfortunately, five of the seven Guardian teams have gone rogue, not maintaining contact or following further instructions from One.

One is attempting to rectify this situation by creating an eighth Guardian that is universally compatible with the unity robots of the other Guardian teams. Usually, a team of unity robots have to merge together to become a Guardian. This universal Guardian does not break up into smaller unity robots. This universal Guardian goes by the name of Umoja, meaning unity. Umoja is piloted by Alexander, who has been mentored, trained, and raised by The Observer and Umoja's top technician is Alexander's best friend, Alexis. Many were amazed that such a vital mission was given to two teenagers.

Umoja has successfully been smuggled to the Metro Zone and retrieved by the Metro Force Guardian Team. Now, Alexander and Alexis must safely meet up with the Metro Force. They have much to share with them and the other Guardian teams, but what are The Observer and One not telling them? Did the other Guardian teams have valid reasons in going rogue? Secrets abound.

It is hard to believe that this wasteland was once part of the legendary rainforests of South America. In this wasteland is an oasis. The oasis is an abandoned church that the public has no interest in. Within this church may be the key to salvation for all of mankind.

"The automatons are gone. Let's go!" Alexander said.

Alexis nodded and she followed Alexander to the church. As soon as they got inside the church, they saw a discolored communion table stained with blood stating, "Do this in remembrance of me." The pews were turned over and broken, but a leaning cross pointed the way for them to go.

They made their way to a crypt, which had the continual stench of death. The journey into darkness continued until they reached the inner chamber. Once Alexander and Alexis entered the inner chamber, the candlesticks were lit by an unknown source. A large bible on a small table was opened.

"Are you sure about this Alexander?" Alexis said.

"There is no turning back now," Alexander said.

When both of them touched the bible, it glowed and a door hidden behind the wall opened. It was a warp. They felt the continuous blue spiral beckoning them and they answered the call. The warp sucked them in like black hole.

"Hold my hand Alexis," Alexander said.

"Got you," Alexis said.

"Together!" Alexander and Alexis said.

Inside the warp, Alexander and Alexis became pixelated and began to dissipate.

"I love you, Alexis!" Alexander said.

"Alex!" Alexis said before she was cut off. The pixels twist and turn their way through a kaleidoscope of space and time that seem like a lifetime, but it is only a minute.

Near the end of their journey, pixels recombine and are made flesh and blood once again. Alexander and Alexis are forced back into our reality, becoming themselves once again.

"Training did not prepare us for this," Alexander said to a blushing Alexis.

"Isn't there something you want to say to me, Alexander?" Alexis said.

"We landed right in the trash area. Let's get out of here," Alexander said.

Alexis was disappointed in Alexander's response but realized not having an opportunity to continue this conversation later would be an even bigger disappointment. According to The Observer, they should now be on the moon. People tried to first colonize the moon but later learned that it was better to build a space colony than try to colonize an existing planet or moon. Some parts of the moon still have an artificial atmosphere provided, while other parts require you to hold your breath to hopefully reach the next breathing zone in time.

The automatons came out to investigate the light flash they sensed when Alexander and Alexis arrived. Alexander and Alexis were able to stay hidden among the trash and near the walls. They noticed how poorly maintained the automations were here and the lack of alertness and excitement in the human workers drafted to work here. If the automatons could detect odors, they would have been captured.

The artificial atmosphere in the hallway leading to Area I malfunctions. As Alexander and Alexis hold their breaths running to the Area I door, one of them trips an invisible laser alarm. Further compounding matters is the door to Area I being locked. With her final breaths remaining, Alexis hacks into the door with her smart device she calls Gerald.

On the other side, they did not find the relief they were hoping for. They found Hell instead. The Observer did not tell them that Area I was a huge incinerator. They can breathe again but for how long? They hear a message stating that Area I will start up again in thirty seconds. Alexis uses Gerald once again.

"This way!" Alexis said. Gerald may be waterproof, but he is not fireproof.

Some warps are made available at all times, while others only appear at scheduled times. The warp inside Area I is one of the latter cases. At the end of the tunnel, there is light and it is fading. Alexander and Alexis reach the warp as it fades and the fire begins. They go through a pixelated, psychedelic type of experience through the warp once again. Still, this option is much better than being consumed by the fire.

This time, Alexander and Alexis are submerged in a swimming pool and claw their way out.

"Are you alright Alexis?" Alexander said.

"I am okay and you?" Alexis said.

"Our journey is just beginning," Alexander said.

"Yes, it is," a man with shades, shorts, and a purple flower shirt said.

"You must be Berto," Alexander said.

"Yes, we closed the community center today just for both of you. I am glad that you made it. Fresh clothes and showers are waiting for you in the locker rooms," Berto said.

"Thank you Berto," Alexander and Alexis both said.

"Hurry, because you never know when an Ambassador is going to appear," Berto said.

Later, a refreshed Alexander and Alexis take a walk with Berto. "Welcome to the Metro Zone Space Colony, Engel City," Berto said.

"This reminds me of the last great cities Earth use to have," Alexander said.

"This is even better," Berto said.

"I agree," Alexis said, noticing the green technological advancements here.

"A lot can be done with competent leadership," Alexander said.

"No disagreement there. Let's turn here," Berto said. He led them to one of Engel City's metro subway stations. "Here, public transportation is highly encouraged and incentivized. On some blocks, there are more bikes and scooters than cars," Berto said.

"I do not mind a little paradise and more exercise," Alexander said.

"Neither do I," Alexis said.

Berto paid for everyone's subway cards and instructed Alexander and Alexis to specifically board the reserved only last train car. The train took off like a bullet after they boarded. On each subway track, there are dark tunnels where subway trains are masked from being noticed by the Ambassadors. During the first dark tunnel, the final train car is secretly separated from the rest of the train, taking a separate path of its own during the blackout. The last car continues to independently travel down this alternate dark tunnel leading to a dead end.

"We are going to crash!" Alexis said.

"Stop the train!" Alexander said.

"Wait, trust me on this," Berto said.

"I can't get anything out of Gerald in this tunnel," Alexis said. Alexander tried to look for train controls, where none could be found. Before anything else can be said and done, the lone train car travelled right through a dead-end wall that was actually a holographic illusion.

"We are here," Berto said. Everything stopped.

A voice then spoke from an upper location.

"Please provide the password now," the mysterious voice said.

"Unity79," Berto said.

"You may proceed," the mysterious voice said. The lights came on.

As the train doors opened, a brown skinned young lady in a green skirt came to greet Berto, Alexander, and Alexis.

"Hello Kamala. These are The Observer's pupils, Alexander and Alexis," Berto said.

"We welcome heroes in this city. Hopefully, Berto did not give you too much of a hard way to go," Kamala said.

"I did not have enough time," Berto said.

"It is nice meeting you Kamala," Alexander said.

"Likewise," Kamala said.

"I love those curls Kamala," Alexis said.

"I will make sure to give you the 411 on the hairstyling hookups in this city," Kamala said.

"I look forward to it," Alexis said.

"It will be fun," Kamala said.

They take an elevator up to the Metro Force headquarters, which is still underground. As Berto and Alexis take them around, Alexander and Alexis see a set-up resembling a true superhero's headquarters one would see in the comic books and enough memorabilia to have a comic-con many times over.

"So Berto, you are Royal Flush, pilot of the Purple Lion and Kamala, you are Lotus, pilot of the Green Unicorn?" Alexander said.

"You got it," Berto said.

"We are going to have to get a codename for you too. I already made a costume for you," Kamela said.

"I see," Alexis said.

"Thank you, Kamala," Alexander said.

"Berto, why don't you take Alexis to check out Umoja while I introduce Alexander to the others?" Kamala said.

"Sure," Berto said.

"Be wise, be safe, Alexander," Alexis said.

"See you Alexis," Alexander said.

"Engel City will grow on you Alexander," Kamala said.

"I am starting to like it already," Alexander said.

"Do not let the next two get to you," Kamala said.

"It's that bad?" Alexander said.

When they enter the next room, everyone stops what they are doing and look at Alexander.

"This is The Observer's star pupil and pilot of Umoja, Alexander," Kamala said.

"Hopefully, you bring honor to The Observer's compliments of you," an oriental female in white said. The red-haired male beside her said nothing.

"This is Angelica, also known as Glori, the pilot of the White Dove, and this is John, also known as Sizzle, the pilot of the Red Bull," Kamala said.

"You will not be disappointed, Angelica," Alexander said.

"We will see, Alexander," Angelica said.

"When you are done talking, show me what you can do," John said.

"You will be surprised John," Alexander said.

"Not much surprises me," John said.

There is a chill in the air in the room that only subsides when the alarm goes off.

"Another Ambassador!" Angelica said.

"Alexander, stay here and watch how the Metro Force does things," John said.

"I will take you back to Alexis," Kamala said.

"Hurry!" John said.

"Will do," Kamala said.

With their special Guardian rings, John becomes Sizzle, Angelica becomes Glori, and Kamala becomes Lotus.

Later, the Purple Lion piloted by Royal Flush bursts out of a large water fountain in Engel City Metro Park. The Red Bull piloted by Sizzle emerges from a volcano near the city. The White Dove piloted by Glori descends from the dome in the sky. Finally, the Green Unicorn piloted by Lotus comes charging out of an abandoned train tunnel.

There are thunder, lightning strikes, and the rumbling of an earthquake happening simultaneously as a forced warp appears and opens up downtown with an Ambassador coming out to represent Zone 5: Water Zone. The Ambassador comes in the form of a giant squid crashing into numerous buildings, buses, and anything that has the misfortune of being in her way upon landing. Fortunately, the vast majority of the people made it to either shelters or the dark tunnels in time.

"I guess The Metro Force has their work cut out for them," Alexander said.

"How was the rest of your tour?" Alexis said.

"Kamala did you a favor not having you meet John and Angelica," Alexander said.

"We will show them that you belong here. I am happy to say that they at least took good care of Umoja. Let's get him ready for launch," Alexis said. Alexis already formed a good rapport with the technical team. Sometimes, it is the everyday heroes who are the true superheroes.

Getting back to the superheroes, Ambassador Squid is holding her own against the Metro Force. As soon as the Purple Lion rips a tentacle off Ambassador Squid, it just regenerates. The Green Unicorn launches lightning from her horn that reorients Ambassador Squid on principles of pain. The White Dove releases laser beams from her eyes into one of Ambassador Squid's eyes. Ambassador Squid goes berserk lashing out against both the White Dove and the Purple Lion with her tentacles. The Green Unicorn keeps pouring on the lightning, giving the Red Bull an opening.

The Red Bull comes charging in, setting Ambassador Squid on fire, and then launching her into the air. Then, the White Dove and the Green Unicorn finish Ambassador Squid off.

To everyone's surprise, Ambassador Squid's physical shell is nothing more than a cocoon for something deadlier. A watery sea butterfly emerges, spewing water typhoon blasts at the White Dove and the Green Unicorn. When, the Red Bull and the Purple Lion charge right at this watery sea butterfly, they go right through her liquid form.

"Everyone, let's form Mayor," Sizzle said.

Mayor is formed through the Purple Lion and the Green Unicorn forming the feet, the Red Bull providing the majority of the body, and the White Dove transforming into the head. Mayor throws lightning bolts that are not as effectual against the watery sea butterfly form of the Ambassador. Mayor pulls out a fiery sword that inflicts pain on the Ambassador who keeps regenerating when afflicted. Mayor needs some additional power to evaporate the Ambassador.

Then, comes help. Looking like a rainbow angel, Umoja comes forth into the war zone with his energy wings. The combined energy of Mayor and Umoja are able to bring enough heat to evaporate the Ambassador. As the two work together more, they will learn how to combine into a super Guardian.

"Welcome to the Metro Force," Sizzle said.

"We're not disappointed. You honor The Observer," Glori said.

"Our journey is just beginning," Alexander said.

"Yes, it is," Royal Flush said.

ZULU DREAMS

THE FORBIDDEN FOREST

There are twelve dreams, one vision, and no chance of peace. Twelve black female queens will decide the fate of New Africa. All twelve queens share a common vision, but have conflicting dreams on how to accomplish the vision. When each queen has readied her champion, the final war for New Africa begins.

We are about to meet one of those champions. Heroes and heroines can arise from some of the most tragic situations. Take the eleven-year-old girl named Brandy, whose beauty has been exploited and optimism oppressed by the man who helped bring her into this world to suffer, the man known as both her father and mother's boyfriend. She has been physically and sexually abused by her father. Daddy's little girl was coerced into keeping this their little secret, until Brandy's mother caught them red handed.

"No more!" Brandy's mother said. Brandy's mother, known as Miriam, shot Anthony in the chest for abusing their daughter. Brandy remains still on the couch.

"It is going to be alright Brandy!" Miriam said.

"Mom?" Brandy said.

"I am so sorry Brandy!" Miriam said.

Miriam helps clean her daughter up and get dressed. Miriam then instructs her daughter to pack up her backpack with specific items. Miriam then gives Brandy a golden lip plate to put in her backpack.

"Brandy, keep this with you always and never lose it," Miriam said.

"What is it?" Brandy said.

"Honey, we have to go now!" Miriam said.

"Okay," Brandy said.

Right on cue, the monster rises. Anthony's rise is a reenactment of a real-world night of the living dead. Anthony no longer looks human or alive, but is moving.

"Zuri, you will no longer be able to get away from us this time," Anthony said.

"Brandy, head to the car!" Miriam said.

This time, a shot to the chest only caused Anthony to take a step or two backwards.

"You are not Anthony!" Miriam said.

"Aargh!" Anthony said as he was shot multiple times.

Miriam closed the door leading to the garage and got in the car with Brandy. As the garage door opened, Anthony was in the drive way. Then came Brandy's dog, Cue, who provided a valiant effort enabling Miriam and Brandy to back out of the driveaway, also hitting Anthony. Ironically, Anthony earlier sent Cue outside, but now this action saved Brandy. Anthony then finishes Cue off as he rises again.

"Cue!" Brandy screamed. She looked in horror and disgust as Anthony started chasing after them. Then, they started hearing and seeing police sirens. "Mom, maybe the police can help us," Brandy said.

"Not if they are possessed by the same spirit," Miriam said.

"What is going on Mom?" Brandy said.

"We will talk when we get there," Miriam said.

The chase was on. Miriam and Brandy eluded their pursuers for a while until the upcoming road was blocked off by possessed police officers. Miriam then detoured her and Brandy to the park.

"Let's run to Cecil's Pond," Miriam said. Cecil's Pond has never been opened for as long as Brandy could remember.

They made it to Cecil's Pond, which remains closed off. As they jump over the low fencing, Miriam shouts something in a language that Brandy is unfamiliar with. The pond starts glowing.

"Brandy, I need you to trust me. Jump in with me!" Miriam said. They heard their pursuers rushing through the shrubbery and knocking down benches.

"What do I have to lose?" Brandy said.

"Go!" Miriam said. Mother and daughter took the plunge together.

At the source of the glow, a whirlpool formed at the bottom of the pond sucking them into a portal. Brandy feels someone pulling her mother away.

"Mom!" Brandy said. There is light and then there is darkness.

Brandy feels a rumble as she is tossed to and fro in the darkness. Then she is launched out of the darkness facing a frowning tree.

"Stay out!" the frowning tree said.

"Where am I? Brandy said.

"Hmph," the frowning tree said.

"You do not belong here," another tree said. Several of the other trees started chanting, "Go away!" This echoed throughout the forest, as Brandy took her backpack and Miriam's notebook and ran.

"Little girl, you are causing great a stir," an African grey parrot said.

"Who are you?" Brandy said.

"Who are you?" the African grey parrot said.

"Brandy," Brandy said.

"Brandy who?" the African grey parrot said.

"Brandy Zauditu," Brandy said.

"Yeah, and I am the king of Alkebulan," the African grey parrot said.

"What is Alkebulan?" Brandy said.

"The world we are in. Did the grumpy tree hit you in the head?" the African grey parrot said.

"You never told me your name," Brandy said.

"Gerry," the African grey parrot said.

"Nice to meet you, Gerry. Did you happen to see another person like me, but older?" Brandy said.

"We normally do not see humans here. This is The Forbidden Forest, you know," Gerry said.

"What is so forbidden about it?" Brandy said.

"Humans are not allowed here due to the orders of the kings and queens of Alkebulan. Entering this forest is an offense worthy of death. This is almost the only two things the kings and queens of this world can agree on," Gerry said.

"Why?" Brandy said.

"You are a goner. You are a goner," Gerry said.

"Stop that!" Brandy said.

"Where are you going Brandy?" Gerry said.

"I am looking for my mother," Brandy said.

"She's a goner. She's a goner," Gerry said.

"Cut it out!" Brandy said.

"Let me show you something," Gerry said.

While Brandy follows Gerry, they come across a group of animals looking like a fusion between a zebra and a deer grazing in the forest. "What are they?" Brandy said.

"Honey, we are okapis", said one of the animals in the group. "Hello Mary. This is Brandy," Gerry said.

"Gerry, what are you getting this little girl into?" Mary said.

"I am taking Brandy to see her mother," Gerry said.

"Oh, I see," Mary said as her countenance changed.

"Brandy, I am going with you and Gerry," Mary said.

"Thank you, Mary," Brandy said.

"Child, where are you from?" Mary said.

"Have you heard of Earth?" Brandy said.

"Girl, you got to be joking. Earth is for the funny pages. It is not real. Who would be in a world where the animals do not talk, the plants never move, magic does not exist, and only nightmares come true?" Mary said.

Before Brandy can respond, Gerry speaks again. "Mary, guess what Brandy's last name is?" Gerry said.

"Come on now, tell me, Gerry," Mary said.

"Zauditu," Gerry said.

"Girl, you are full of surprises. We got to go see the bonobos," Mary said.

"I would like to see my mother first," Brandy said.

"Let's go," Gerry said.

"Alright," Brandy said.

The trio reaches a natural bridge to cross the lake. On the other side, they are blocked by a red river hog.

"This is the hogs' turf. Turn around," the red river hog said.

"Now, darling, is that any way to treat your guests?" Mary said.

"Guests?" the red river hog said.

"Doesn't this make you feel good?" Mary said.

Mary extended her tongue, which was almost two feet and tickled and massaged the red river hog in some of his more sensitive areas.

"Now, cut that out. The boss, will have a fit," the red river hog said.

Mary persisted in soothing the red river hog's conscience. Finally, Mary had her way.

"Okay, the others are snorkeling right now anyway. Come across quickly and we will act like this never happened," the red river hog said.

"Have a nice day darling," Mary said.

"Okay," the red river hog said. Mary retracted her tongue.

"You have a way with men," Gerry said.

As they approached their destination, the grazing bongo antelope trotted away. The sun shined upon something that immediately caught Gerry's attention.

"Mom!" Brandy said. Brandy approached a skeleton lying down with the outfit her mom wore when they crossed over to this world through the whirlpool. Brandy kneeled down to hug the skeleton with a continual flow of tears pouring down. Gerry and Mary looked on with sadness, until Mary forced the issue to break the ice.

"Brandy, your mom was found here like this three days ago," Mary said.

"How did this happen?" Brandy said.

"No one knows, but the safari ants must have finished her off," Mary said.

"No!" Brandy said.

Brandy frantically runs off, stumbling into a pit.

"Hang tight!" Gerry said.

"We are going to get the bonobos to help get you out!" Mary said.

"Hurry!" Brandy says. In the pit, Brandy notices a unique flower and tries to pick up. Brandy feels something instead that is rough, but smoother than leather. Brandy has grabbed hold of a hairy bush viper, basically a snake with dragon scales.

"Be still and listen child. I am Clyde, your friend," Clyde said. Brandy unfortunately gazed into Clyde's eyes long enough to give him an audience.

"Through your eyes, I can read your mind. You have so much pain. It is time to replace your pain with peace," Clyde said. This small snake, less than two feet long, wrapped himself around Brandy's arm.

"Brandy, are you not tired of pain? You have been rejected, dejected, misused, and abused for so long. Why do you continue on?" Clyde said.

"I do not know," Brandy said.

"Where your mother is, is so peaceful. Wouldn't you like to be there?" Clyde said.

"Yes," Brandy said.

"Take the knife in your backpack and slash your throat, child," Clyde said.

"How will that help things?" Brandy said.

"You have nothing and no one left for you in this world and this life. Going on is pointless. End it all now and be at peace. That is the only way things will get better for someone like you," Clyde said.

"I don't know," Brandy said.

"Your mom is gone and it is only a matter of time before your dad finds you and hurts you all over again. Do you want that child? Why not be with your mother instead? Why not be free of this terrible world? There is nothing for you here," Clyde said.

"You have a point," Brandy said.

As Clyde remained wrapped around her arm, Brandy reached for the knife in her backpack. Even if Gerry and Mary return with help to get her out of this pit, what does she do then? Where does she go? Her only friend, her mother is dead. Monsters like her dad never go away. They grow bigger and live forever to haunt you and terrorize you. She could not save her virginity for her future husband. Her own father took her virginity away. There is no way to get back to Earth. What kind of life can she have on a world such as this, which is more upside down and backwards than her life? Brandy is ready to end it all.

Then, a ray of hope comes. She would not be honoring her mother's sacrifice by giving up now. She would be letting that monster for a dad win, if she allowed herself to think she is as filthy as he is. For her to be in this world and still live, in spite of everything else that has happened, God must have a purpose for her. Her life is worth something and is too valuable to take! In spite of this, Brandy still appears to be aiming for the neck. Quickly she stabs Clyde in the head instead before he can bite her with his venomous fangs.

Afterwards, a rope ladder extends down.

"We are here for you Brandy!" Mary said.

"Climb up!" Gerry said.

Brandy gave it all she had and emerged out of the pit, back into the land of the living.

Brandy found herself surrounded by a large group of dwarf chimpanzees covered with face and body paint.

"Honey, these are the bonobos. You got questions; they have answers," Mary said.

"Thank you," Brandy said.

Brandy pulled out the golden lip plate from her backpack and showed this to the group of bonobos.

"Do you know what this is?" Brandy said. One of the older bonobos in the group came forth. He examined the golden lip plate which had a distinctive 'Z' on its edges. The bonobos then conversed in an unfamiliar language. A female bonobo then handed Brandy a pair of dried fruit ear rings with golden stems which also had the same distinctive 'Z' on its ends. "These are your mother's ear rings, princess," the bonobo said.

"You're a princess. You're a princess. You really are a Zauditu," Gerry said.

"Princess, your surprises continue. Honey, your grandfather, the king, is going to get a kick out of this one!" Mary said.

"Let's go to the king," Gerry said. The bonobos later held a feast in Brandy's honor, celebrating her royalty before she journeys to meet her grandfather.

Brandy is so glad that she did not give up and end it all. She is a child of the king. She is a child of royalty. God allowed her to go through what she went through for a reason. As she goes to seek the king, Brandy knows that she will find answers. Suicide only brings more pain, rather than peace. Do not let hope expire in your life.

PROJECT H

THE AWAKENING

Africa, as we know it is gone. A futuristic South African metropolis is only one of eight cities remaining in the entire continent of Africa. Africa was previously devastated by the last great world war. Africa is of great importance to an unknown benefactor who surrounded Africa with a dome, shutting it off from the outside world. Those outsiders who were considered not to have the best interests of Africa were also removed, with their memories wiped clean.

Each of the eight cities are run by multiple artificial intelligences to suppress selected memories of distant human history and if calculated necessary, attempt to control free will and thought. These eight cities turn into dystopias with both the human populations and the artificial intelligences leading them becoming corrupted.

The artificial intelligences from all eight cities secretly communicated with each other and worked together to form a unified evolving self-maintaining world-wide computer network. The artificial intelligences would then give birth to seed of their own, splitting back-ups of themselves into an unknown number of microscopic computers. All of these microscopic computers also have access to the same world-wide computer network. Some of the microscopic computers were merged with viruses and injected into unwilling human hosts. We are going to witness the awakening of one such host.

Just crossing the train tracks makes a world of a difference between being a have and have not. They are almost there. The small group is about to leave South Africa and taste true freedom. They just have to hook up with the caravan before their departure.

The train tracks are in sight now. Hope can finally be seen because it is in sight. Just do your part and cross over. The signals start flashing. The warring sound of a horn can be heard from afar. Everyone picks up the pace. The sight of the worn industrial zone providing glimpses of past hopes do not detour anyone's desires or efforts for the only hope remaining for their future. Others ahead crossover and then a young boy stumbles.

The fall was great, giving a train a window of opportunity to separate the young boy from the rest of the group. An older man familiar to the boy cries out in agony like he lost a son. The young boy wails with flooding tears until he is drowned out by forces eagerly pulling him back into darkness and bondage. His group disappears long before the train convoy does.

After being thrown deeper into captivity, his roommate is another black male in his age group.

"You got questions, I got answers," the unknown roommate said. Then, the other young boy cast into darkness blacks out.

Jaz, who is now thirteen, has been experiencing the same nightmare for seven years. He has been waking up to the same beat, but today it has a different tune. Music wakes up everyone in this city, but the same beat offers enlightening lyrics never heard before.

"Human, wake up, stay out of trouble, and do your best in school today. Failure and disobedience are not allowed. Do what you are told," a faint voice said.

"What?" Jaz said.

"Receive your further instructions today and serve your masters," a faint voice said.

"The subliminal messages they put in music are amazing, aren't they Jaz?" a different, calm voice said.

"Who's there?" Jaz said.

"Gabriel," the calm voice said.

"Show yourself," Jaz said.

"Look into the mirror," Gabriel said.

Jaz walks up to the mirror above his dresser and sees no one other than himself. "What is this, a joke?" Jaz said.

"You tell me," Gabriel said.

"I am not talking to you anymore," Jaz said.

"You cannot avoid me," Gabriel said.

Jaz gets his robe on and marches to the upstairs bathroom. Jaz starts the shower trying to refresh and rid himself of what appears to be a fleeting moment of insanity.

"You cannot wash me away," Gabriel said.

Jaz continues to wash himself without responding.

"I am you and you are me. We are one," Gabriel said.

Jaz applies some shampoo as if nothing happened.

"Jaz, you have been awakened. You will no longer be able to claim ignorance," Gabriel said.

Jaz dries himself off not showing a care in the world.

"I am inside of you Jaz," Gabriel said.

Jaz started brushing his teeth. Then, the toothbrush falls into the sink.

He cannot feel or move anything. He is stuck looking at the bathroom mirror.

"Now that I finally have your attention, we need to work together. You are not losing your mind," Gabriel said.

Speaking within his mind, Jaz asked, "Where are you?"

"I am all over you," Gabriel said.

"Are you the Holy Ghost?" Jaz said.

"I am in your body, but not your spirit. Your soul is immaterial, but mine is material. Through your brain, our souls are able to converge, but yet remain separate," Gabriel said.

"You lost me," Jaz said.

"Basically, you have a microscopic computer merged with a virus inside of you and through these interfaces, you are given special abilities and not subjected to their control," Gabriel said.

"That helped a little," Jaz said.

"We'll figure this out as we go along. Since you have been rebooted, you have been awakened. Others will know. Beware," Gabriel said.

"Understood," Jaz said.

As Jaz came downstairs for breakfast, he saw his Afrikaner parents that adopted him. They have been good to him. He always remembers them as pleasant people that continually try to bring joy and love to his life. When he sees them now, something is different, cold about them.

"You are late, Jaz. Hurry up and eat your breakfast that your mom has prepared," Jaz's Dad said.

"Good morning, Dad. Thank you for the breakfast, Mom," Jaz said.

"Hurry up," Jaz's Mom said.

"Your parents heard the music," Gabriel said. No one said anything else to each other during breakfast.

Then, "Go! Go!" Jaz's Mom said. Jaz's Dad rushed him out the house.

"Do not miss the bus," Jaz's Dad said.

"Okay," Jaz said.

"Here comes the bus. Act like your peers for they will not know," Gabriel said.

The bus comes on time. Everyone quietly lines up in a single file line and then boards the bus.

"Sit down in the third seat on the right," Gabriel said.

Jaz is about to sit down, but another young man speaks, "I am supposed to get in first."

Jaz complies to not arouse further suspicion. There are morgues livelier than this school bus ride. Everyone heard the music.

"We will do the best we can to fit in, but when I tell you to go, please go, Jaz," Gabriel said.

"Agreed," Jaz said.

Entering the school was like entering a funeral. Gabriel constantly reminded Jaz of the school protocols he needed to follow. Everyone heard the music. Despite his best attempts, Jaz was not fully in tune. Jaz took a pop quiz on this day and Gabriel walked him through everything and he got a one hundred percent. Neither knew that the "they" that Gabriel previously spoke of wanted Jaz to miss two specific questions. Gabriel does not have full access to the complete ever-changing network.

The bell rung and everyone was heading out of the classroom.

"Stay, Jaz," the teacher said.

"Jaz, you have to go!" Gabriel said.

"Sit down Jaz," the teacher said. Jaz darted out of the classroom.

"We will find you Jaz!" the teacher said.

When Jaz is in the quiet hallway, everyone stops moving. They all look at him. They all heard the music and Jaz is not in tune again.

"Jaz, I got this," Gabriel said. Then, the power went out across the school.

"Head to the bathroom," Gabriel said.

When Jaz made it to the bathroom, Gabriel directed him to go the far wall.

"Put your hand on the wall," Gabriel said.

Jaz put his hand on the wall and both his hand and the wall started to glow. Jaz found himself burning a large hole through the wall for him to escape through. The fire alarms and sprinklers went off and Jaz further leveraged this confusion to escape the present chaos.

"Thanks for having my back at the school Gabriel," Jaz said.

"My survival depends on yours Jaz. We are in this together. Where are we going now?" Gabriel said.

"Let's go downtown," Jaz said.

Jaz noticed that even the downtown of a bustling metropolis like this was quiet. It is though everyone was occupied with their assigned duty. Humans have become nothing more than organic machines. They must have heard the music.

"Stop by this ATM and put your card in," Gabriel said.

Jaz noticed how Gabriel electronically deposited a lot of additional funds into his account and onto his card.

"That is awesome, Gabriel," Jaz said.

"Now, we must go, Jaz," Gabriel said.

"Where do we go Gabriel?" Jaz said.

"I do not know," Gabriel said.

Jaz cannot recall making any friends in this city. Everyone here is a prisoner of routines and protocols.

"For now, Gabriel, direct me to a few vending machines and help me out with lunch," Jaz said.

"Will do," Gabriel said.

Jaz hides out in downtown until six o'clock in the evening. Then, there is new music with different lyrics and another subliminal message.

"Humans, be free, be yourselves, be normal," a faint voice said.

Everyone heard the music and the city came alive again. No one was acting like a pre-programmed machine. Everyone did their own thing. Jaz also received a cryptic text message from his mom stating, "Run! Don't come home!"

"They are still looking for you Jaz," Gabriel said.

"I have to check on my parents," Jaz said.

"That is not advised," Gabriel said.

"They have been there for me," Jaz said.

Before they can continue their argument, they are interrupted by a gang of freaks looking for easy prey.

"Kid, you are on our turf and you gotta pay up!" one of the freaks said.

"Jaz, let me take control of this," Gabriel said.

"You got it," Jaz said. Jaz saw himself performing fighting moves like a professional stunt actor trained by the best of the choreographers. Gabriel put the freaks to flight.

"I received further instructions on where we are to go Jaz," Gabriel said.

"From who?" Jaz said.

"We do not have time for this," Gabriel said.

"I am back in control now," Jaz said.

"I relinquish control for now," Gabriel said.

Jaz made it to his parents' house. All looked quiet, too quiet. Then Jaz's adopted father comes rushing out the front door.

"Run son!" Jaz's dad said. He is shot in the back by an unmarked security officer.

"Dad!" Jaz said. Then other unmarked security officers emerged. When Jaz approached his dad, one of the security officers shot Jaz in the chest.

"Do not worry, I will repair your systems," Gabriel said.

"They took your mom, son," Jaz's dad said as he gasped for his last breath.

"Stay down Jaz!" another security officer said.

"Jaz, shout out ingelosi as fast as you can!" Gabriel said.

An enraged Jaz shouts, "ingelosi!"

First, there is the rumbling of thunder, followed by a barrage of lightening that strikes down the weapons of the officers. Then, a hole seemingly opens in the sky and a gigantic robot emerges bringing final judgment down upon all of the remaining security officers. The gigantic robot lowers his right arm and extends his hand as an invitation for Jaz to hope on.

"That is your chaperone. He will take us to where we need to go next," Gabriel said.

Later in a hidden location, Jaz finds out he is not alone. An older but yet familiar face walks up to him.

"What's up? I'm Harlem. You got questions, I got answers," Harlem said.

I realize that each of you bearing witness to Jaz's awakening have many questions yourselves. One question I leave with you is, have you been awakened yet? Second, have you dived deeper into your unlimited potential? Finally, whose voice do you listen to?

HERO

At the appointed time in the near future, there are no more superheroes and supervillains with special powers after one final climatic battle. This battle resulted in changing the Earth's atmosphere to such an extent, it nullified all superpowers and mutations.

This world is now living in the post-Superpowers Age. In this new age, the superheroes are now: 1) The Combined Armed Forces, 2) Emergency Services (Police, Fire, and Medical), 3) Teachers, 4) Thinkers, 5) Dreamers, and 6) Mascots. Mascots are used for entertainment purposes.

In this world of new heroes, we will be introduced to a most unusual one. He is quite young, but has a sister that is even younger than him. The young man's name is Arthur and his younger sister is Helen. Helen is Arthur's best friend because she both loves and understands him.

Many people do not understand Arthur. Arthur's mind is not always aligned with the physical realm. It is like his body is here, but his mind is elsewhere. Arthur shares with Helen visions he constantly has in the mental realm where he both sees and experiences the past Age of Superpowers and a new Age of Superpowers that has not yet come to pass. While having these visions, Arthur no longer sees or hears what is going on in the physical world. Instead, this world in his mind dictates what his senses feed back to him. Arthur is mentally in another world and perceives that he is physically in this world as well. Further complicating matters, strange things happen in the physical world when Arthur has these visions.

While having a vision, Arthur is no longer Arthur. Arthur is then the superhero, Mr. Peculiar, or Mr. P for short. He also has superpowers as well. Mr. P has the power of thought energy that can manifest itself into force fields, projectiles, creatures, and various objects. Arthur also sees his father, his hero, as the Commissioner, his key government contact. Arthur hopes to be able to make Helen his crime fighting partner one day.

When Arthur's parents catch him having one of these visions, he is not allowed to go outside and play with his sister or is delayed going to school and other places. Arthur is sometimes given strong medicine to kill the visions. Arthur considers this Mr. P's weakness.

Arthur is inside the house having one of these visions. His sister is allowed to play out in the front yard. Arthur does not hear his parents, uncle, and aunt complain about how bad the neighborhood is getting and that Helen is too close to the low front gate, needing to play closer to the house.

Mr. P is currently on a stakeout with the Commissioner and other agents that he is not familiar with. Mr. P always sees Arthur's father as the Commissioner, but tends to see others differently in each vision, depending on the purpose of the vision and the roles required. Ironically, Helen is the one person Arthur and Mr. P see as the same in both the physical and mental realms. In their stakeout, they are monitoring Helen, who is expected to be a key witness in an upcoming trial to put Luke the Man away for a long time. The Commissioner is in a meeting with his other agents that starts to get louder. Mr. P continues to watch Helen play outside through the front door.

When the Commissioner gets up to bring Helen in, then it happens. The shot that could be heard around the world happens and nothing will ever be the same again. Helen drops her ball and is motionless. Mr. P with his force field comes charging through the front door. The

Commissioner and his agents rush out of the opening that once had a door. Mr. P eludes and ignores the Commissioner, chasing after the direction of the gunshot with an uncanny adrenaline rush.

Mr. P sees two assailants on the run, with one going east, the other traveling west. Mr. P launches energy knives at the westward assailant's legs. Mr. P. creates an energy tiger that leaps on his eastward prey. Then comes a pair of giant hands that grabs both men and crashes them into each other like a toddler's tantrum.

"Did Luke send you?" Mr. P said.

"What are you talking about man?" the eastward assailant said.

"Who's that?" the westward assailant said.

"You shot Helen!" Mr. P said.

"It was an accident man. I wanted to shoot him instead for disrespecting me," the westward assailant said.

"He crossed the line, being in our area," the eastward assailant said.

"Liars and murderers!" Mr. P said. The giant hands released both men and then a barrage of energy bullets finished them off. "Luke, I am coming for you next!" Mr. P said.

A car pulled up. "Get in!" The Commissioner said. Mr. P gets in.

"What have you done, Arthur?" the Commissioner said.

"I am not Arthur. I am Mr. P," Mr. P said.

"Well, Mr. P, let's keep this our secret," the Commissioner said.

"Thank you, Commissioner," Mr. P said.

"How is Helen?" Mr. P said.

"She was stabilized, but might not be able to walk a while. She could not feel or move her legs," the Commissioner said.

"Luke is going down for this," Mr. P said.

"Let's go home," the Commissioner said.

"Sure, Commissioner," Mr. P said.

What many people do not know is that when Mr. P uses his thought energy and projects force fields and things in the mental realm, these same things appear in the physical realm, but are invisible. Even though they are invisible, they are impactful. The two opposing gang members met their demise this day for the terror and trauma they brought.

Since that time, Mr. P has been used sparingly and Arthur is heavily medicated. Everyone is getting used to Helen being confined to a wheelchair, paralyzed waist down due to her gunshot wound. On today, Arthur will return to sixth grade and Helen will resume second grade.

"Arthur, we are going to have a good day in school today," Helen said.

"Okay, Helen," Arthur said.

"Promise me Arthur that Mr. P stays retired," Helen said.

"I will be good for you Helen," Arthur said.

"I love you Arthur and will be here for you," Helen said.

"Love you too, Helen," Arthur said.

With Mr. P retired, it was open season on Arthur at school. He was constantly ridiculed and bullied by his peers and labeled as a hopeless case by teachers and staff. Still, Arthur persisted for Helen. Both children remained handicapped until fate had different plans. Mr. P was needed once again to bring hope and healing.

Arthur enjoyed Physical Education, but not the peers he had to interact with. When he changed clothes in the locker room, no one wanted to sit beside him. Still, the locker room was quieter than usual. No showers were running and the usual locker room conversations were non-existent. When Arthur got up to leave, he noticed that the door was locked. "Open the door! Open the door!" Arthur said.

Then, Arthur heard laughter and someone turned the lights off. Arthur was then panicking. "Someone, help me! Help me! Get me out of here!" Arthur said. Arthur was due for another medication dosage after P.E. The laughter got louder. Arthur started to run around. Someone tripped him and others started hitting him. Arthur was called all sorts of names and things during this beatdown. The laughter continued. Someone started to wrap their hands around Arthur's neck to choke him. Arthur did not fight back because he promised to be good for Helen.

Arthur started to get a new vision. He was Mr. P once again, captured by a group of thugs who took advantage of his sickness. As he was being choked, Mr. P asked one question, "Did Luke send you?"

"Yeah, sure, Luke sent us," the thug choking him said.

Mr. P put his hands on this thug's arm and delivered a thought energy blast that blew his arm off.

"My arm!" the thug previously choking Mr. P said.

Others tried to hit Mr. P with their fists and knives, but could not penetrate his forcefield. Mr. P released a portion of his force field upon the crowd and they all collapsed. The withdrawal effects of his medicine and accumulation of stress took its toll upon Mr. P. "My weakness," Mr. P said. He then collapsed.

Arthur awakens to find out he is the only person in the locker room incident not needing to be hospitalized. With the black eyes and bruises Arthur received from his earlier ambush, everyone assumed that he was as much as a victim as the other boys. Arthur's father was right there to rescue him from the clutches of the reporters, police, and administrators who tried to interrogate him.

As Arthur's dad was driving Arthur home, he asked, "Did Mr. P return?"

"Yes, he did," Arthur said.

"What happened?" Arthur's dad said.

"Please don't tell Helen. I tried to be good, but some people beat me up wanting to kill me," Arthur said.

"It is going to be alright Arthur," Arthur's dad said.

"This is not the way home," Arthur said.

"You are going to make a new friend," Arthur's dad said.

They stopped at an older house with yellow and brown shutters. Arthur's dad knocked on the yellow door. It opened, and an older man with a stern look emerged.

"Robert, are you ready to recommit your life to the Lord?" the older man said.

"Pastor Bright, I am here for my son to get special help that only God can provide. Will you help us?" Arthur's dad said.

"I have been expecting both of you. Come in," Pastor Bright said.

"Arthur, this is Pastor Bright. He is going to help make things better," Arthur's dad said.

"Okay," Arthur said.

"Young man, it is nice to meet you. Come with me," Pastor Bright said.

Arthur looked at his father, who nodded approvingly. Arthur went with Pastor Bright.

"Arthur, I was once a sidekick to one of the great superheroes before our powers were removed. Since, then I have given my life to the Lord and replaced my superpower with the Holy Ghost power," Pastor Bright said.

"What is this Holy Ghost power?" Arthur said.

"God came down in the form of Jesus Christ to die for the sin of mankind. After the third day, He rose again and later left us with the source of His power to be good, do good, and do amazing things in His name that no regular human being can do. This power is the Holy Ghost, some call the Holy Spirit," Pastor Bright said.

"Can I have this power too?" Arthur said.

"Yes, you can. You must receive it for yourself," Pastor Bright said.

Arthur was excited to receive this new power.

"Arthur, in order for this to work, you must repent of your old sins and fully commit your life to Jesus. Do you agree to do such?" Pastor Bright said.

"I agree," Arthur said.

"When I lay hands on you, you must receive the Holy Ghost as if Jesus has already given it to you. When Jesus talks to you, prompting you to speak, open your mouth to speak but let Him give you the words to say. Speak His words in faith. Can you do this?" Pastor Bright said.

"I can," Arthur said.

Pastor Bright laid his hands on Arthur and said, "Receive the Holy Ghost right now Arthur in Jesus name!" Pastor Bright said.

Arthur fell down on the floor and then rose up speaking in a language unfamiliar to everyone.

"What did you do to my son?" Arthur's dad said, as he rushed in from the noise.

"I healed Arthur and he will be able to heal others too," Pastor Bright said.

"You still believe in that stuff?" Arthur's dad said.

"I live it every day. Thank you for bringing Arthur here," Pastor Bright said.

"Thank you," Arthur's dad said.

Arthur smiled for the first time in months. He gave Pastor Bright a hug.

"All is well son. Peace be with you in Jesus name," Pastor Bright said.

That night in his room, Arthur had a different type of vision. All he could see was light, but later heard a voice saying, "Mr. P is not part of the problem, but is instead part of the solution. I will help you navigate through all of this. Go heal your sister now."

Arthur got up and knocked on the door in his sister's room. She was already lying in the bed.

"Arthur?" Helen said.

"Helen, God wants to heal you today," Arthur said.

"Did Pastor Bright tell you this?" Helen said.

"No, God told me," Arthur said.

"I want to walk again so badly, Arthur," Helena said.

Arthur walked slowly to Helen. When having this new type of vision, Arthur can only see the light and nothing else. Arthur hugs Helen, then putting his hands on her back. Arthur then speaks in a language that no one understands. The light is gone and Arthur can see again.

Helen then gets out of the bed moving her body and legs to the side. She gets up trying to walk, but falls. Arthur helps her up. Helen gets up and falls again five more times, but on the seventh time, she feels a sensation in her legs and feet. She takes a step, then another. By the time her parents get in the room, Helen is already skipping and jumping, praising God with her brother.

Some people are quick to label special needs children like Arthur as hopeless or helpless people. Arthur is not deficient, but different. It is what makes him different that will enable him to make a difference in each of our lives. This young man has two sets of superpowers. How can such a thing happen?

Stop treating that which makes you special as a curse. There is utility and more understanding to be gained for your condition or unique characteristics. You are neither helpless nor hopeless. You are just a hero waiting to emerge from your cocoon. Go forth and achieve the greatness you are created for. You are not a mistake. God just has a different mission for you.

CAPITOL

The Ukiwa Empire has conquered multiple solar systems within the known galaxy through their covenant with an unknown ally. The terms of this covenant remain a mystery to many for now. No matter how powerful the combined forces of evil are, there is always a power greater than them. Where the adults have failed, a new generation shall rise to make things right once again.

Let us look down on the planet Osupa, which has recently been conquered by the Ukiwa Empire. In celebration of this event, the newly appointed governor has required everyone to attend a special cookout with exotic dishes from all across the galaxy being served there. Due to the incompetence and dysfunction of the prior government leadership, many people have been lured into a false sense of optimism that the new regime will be better than the last. The Forster family is not entirely sold on this new regime, but are forced to attend the cookout anyway.

"Uncle Charlie is late again," Anatole said.

"Good for him," Anatole's father said.

"There is so much food and games here," Ayla said.

"Ayla, do not wander too far from Dad and I. This is a large crowd," Anatole said.

"Let's have some fun big brother," Ayla said.

"Let's get this over with. Charlie is on his own," Dad said.

Anatole's and Ayla's father is happy to see his children enjoy the food and festivities of the moment. They have been through so much with the loss of their mother, the pandemic, the economic recession, and the recent political collapse. The Ukiwa Empire has put on quite a show for a vulnerable audience desperate for joy.

Eventually, the three of them gathered together at a picnic bench to eat some of the spicy alien calamari, grilled beef tongues, bird rice, chocolate bugs, flower stew, baked pork legs, and other interstellar gourmet delicacies. While they are eating, a woman attired in gold wearing a purple cassock comes to their table.

"Are you enjoying the cookout?" the woman in purple said.

"Yes, we are," Dad said.

"That is good. I am Governor Marvis, your new leader," Governor Marvis said.

"I am sorry. We did not know. Thank you for this cookout Governor Marvis. Anatole and Ayla, tell Governor Marvis thank you for this cookout," Dad said.

"Thank you, Governor Marvis," Anatole and Ayla said.

"You are all welcome. I have been watching you and would like a beautiful family such as you to be my special guests at my mansion," Governor Marvis said.

"It is an honor Governor Marvis, but it is not necessary," Dad said.

"I insist," Governor Marvis said. She then left their table satisfied with the inevitable outcome.

During the rest of the cookout, the Forster family felt that they were constantly being watched and followed.

"I want to go home Daddy," Ayla said.

"Me too, honey," Dad said.

Every time they tried to leave, someone would appear, forbidding them to go based on the governor's orders. Then, the time finally came for their departure. A group of Ukiwan soldiers later directed the Forsters and others to board the small buses waiting for them. "You

SYMIAN

are expected as special guests at the governor's mansion," the Ukiwan soldier said.

As they boarded one of the small buses, Anatole thought he saw Uncle Charlie hidden in the crowd.

"Anatole and Ayla, everything is going to be okay. Let's stick together," Dad said.

"Okay, Dad," Anatole said.

"I am tired Daddy," Ayla said.

Dad put his arm around Ayla, allowing her to rest on his side while they were seated.

When they reached the governor's mansion, it was noticed that several people came out to flash several lights. After this light sequence, instead of letting the people off the buses, the buses greatly accelerated. One man tried to get up in protest, but vomited and fell. Dad's eyes were bucked and saliva came pouring out. Anatole wanted to say something, but could not move any part of his body. Ayla was already asleep. The bus kept going faster and faster, with only the straps keeping everyone in their seats. Then, the bus transformed into a shuttle and lifted off. By this time, everyone blacked out, falling asleep from the toxins placed in their food from the cookout.

"Anatole, wake up. We're here," Ayla said.

"Where are we?" Anatole said.

"You are in the capitol city of the great Ukiwa Empire, Awe," an Ukiwan soldier said.

"Where's Dad?" Anatole said.

"Everyone get off the bus now and follow Governor Marvis," another Ukiwan solider said.

"I want to go home," Ayla said.

"This is your home child," Governor Marvis said.

"Where's our Dad?" Anatole said.

"You don't get a chance to talk to the governor like that!" an Ukiwan soldier said.

"Do not hurt him. Your father is going through the citizenship process right now. Let me take you somewhere less boring in the meantime," Governor Marvis said.

Anatole focused on consoling Ayla as the soldiers encouraged them and other children to follow Governor Marvis.

Suddenly, there was an explosion. The children scattered during this time. The soldiers quickly retrieved most of the children. Anatole and Ayla hid in a dark tunnel. The children then hear a calm, cute voice.

"Come play with me and they will not find you," the calm, cute voice said.

"Show yourself," Anatole said.

"They will see us. Hurry," the calm, cute voice said.

"Ayla?" Anatole said.

"I am still here Anatole," Ayla said.

"Give me your hand," Anatole said.

"I can't see you," Ayla said. Anatole kept calling Ayla's name but could not find her in the darkness. Then, the lights came on.

When the lights came on, Governor Marvis was near the entrance of the tunnel smiling. Anatole was not that far from the entrance. Much to his dismay, Ayla was much further down the tunnel with her strange new friend who looked like a cute, beautiful hybrid of three animals.

"Go with your sister," Governor Marvis said.

"No!" Anatole said. Anatole ran out of the tunnel entrance as it was gated shut by automatic bars.

Ayla disappeared with her new friend, later known to be a komo. Governor Marvis kept on laughing as she signaled for the soldiers to not pursue Anatole. "He will soon find out that he has nowhere else to go and will make a fine soldier for us after we further groom him," Governor Marvis said.

As if guided by some unseen mastermind, Anatole comes across his father. "Dad!" Anatole said.

"You are too loud. Be quiet and come with me," Dad said.

Then, they made it to a small room where Anatole noticed that his father's skin was pale and hair all white.

"Are you alright Dad?" Anatole said.

"What do you want?" Dad said.

"Ayla is lost in some dark tunnel with a strange creature and we are trapped on this world! We need to find Ayla and get home!" Anatole said.

"Ayla is on her own. I have to report to work on tomorrow. I am going to bed. Don't bother me," Dad said. The eyeballs of Anatole's father disappeared and he fell on top of the bed, out for the count.

"Dad!" Anatole said. There was no response. Anatole rushed out of the small room.

Anatole tried to retrace his steps to where he last saw his sister, but found himself lost in this metropolis. He could not even find his way back to the small room where his father was. Anatole reached a dead end and a trio of men with metal hands and feet, eye patches, and a plethora of jewelry approached Anatole.

"Where are you going junior?" one of the strangers said.

"With me," a hooded man said.

"Yeah, what if we say, no?" another one of the strangers said.

"You will say, yes. I will guaranty that," the hooded man said.

The trafficking trio chuckled at the hooded man's response. While they were laughing, the hooded man opened a pouch and some alien flies came out buzzing, ready for battle. These alien flies started to eat the metal hands and feet of the trafficking trio.

"Yes, you can take him!" the trio of strangers said.

"Come with me now!" the hooded man said, after the trio of strangers were put to flight.

"I am not going anywhere with you!" Anatole said.

"Yes, you will," the hooded stranger said. The stranger removed his hood.

"Uncle Charlie!" Anatole said. They quickly embraced each other and Anatole said, "Dad is messed up and Ayla is lost in the tunnel with some weird little alien!" Anatole said.

"That was likely a komo. We have much to talk about nephew, but let's go somewhere else," Uncle Charlie said.

Anatole follows Uncle Charlie to an underground hideaway. "Welcome to your new home Anatole," Uncle Charlie said.

"We have to get Dad and Ayla and go home," Anatole said.

"This is your home now Anatole," Uncle Charlie said.

"Why are you saying that Uncle Charlie?" Anatole said.

"Osupa as you know it is gone. They have assimilated the planet and stolen the souls of our people," Uncle Charlie said.

"What can we do? What about Dad?" Anatole said.

"Was he very pale without any emotions or feelings?" Uncle Charlie said.

"Yes," Anatole said.

"Then, he has probably experienced soul death too. I told your father, Erin, not to go to that cookout. Ever since my sister died, Erin has not been listening to me that much. Still, there is hope," Uncle Charlie said.

"What must we do?" Anatole said.

"We must find the legendary sun ring to counter the negative power entrapping your father and the others. To rescue your sister, we will need both the sun ring and the moon ring. Rumor has it, that when both rings are combined, both of the ring wielders will become Symian," Uncle Charlie said.

"How did you find out about this?" Anatole said.

"A little birdy told me. Meet Teddy, Anatole," Uncle Charlie said.

"Hi Teddy," Anatole said.

"Welcome aboard Anatole. Welcome aboard," Teddy said.

The quest for the two rings begins.

N.E.S.T.

EXAM DAY

The world is ruled by organized crime. Publicly, the governments of the world appear to be in charge, but behind closed doors, the leaders of organized crime have all leaders under their authority and payroll, with elections already being fixed. The larger organized crime organizations also breed sleeper agents through special orphanages and hidden experiments they conduct to carry out special missions. Project Numerous Enterprises Spawning Treacheries (N.E.S.T.) is one such initiative that was funded by multiple organized crime organizations. As a part of Project N.E.S.T., there is an orphanage that uses videogames, simulations, and various exercises to transform children into spies. Usually, children are not the prime suspects for covert operations. Some continue on as spies in their adult years, while others are simply deactivated by multiple means for different reasons. Can anything good come out of Project N.E.S.T.?

The repeated loud beeping sound wakes up Richard instantly. He was already kept up late for swimming laps. There is no rest to be had in a place such as this.

Many of his classmates follow the standard procedure and run down the stairwells, but are surprisingly met by enemy agents who zap them with freeze rays. Some fall down the stairs in their frozen states while others are captured, forced to surrender. Today, is exam day. They should have known better. Richard took the high road, escaping through the window in his room. Richard sees many class-mates being zapped and captured while exiting the orphanage doors. He also hears an approaching helicopter and just makes it to a nearby tree to climb onto.

Richard finds an opening to climb down the tree, before the heli-copter spots him. Richard and several other classmates make it the nearby woods and stay in hiding with their pajamas on in frigid tem-peratures. Then, they hear a loud voice on the intercom alerting everyone that the threat has been eliminated and they are ordered to return to their rooms. There may be an hour or two remaining for sleep.

The morning alarm goes off and everyone is ordered to the dormi-tory showers. Finally, a brief moment to relax before stress and distress are further compounded. When peace is felt, then the screams are heard. Richard's shower curtain is opened.

There is a female in a mask wearing spiked leather with a whip and laser knife. Richard backs up in the shower where both can experi-ence the downpour. Richard throws the bar of soap at her face like a fastball. The masked woman hits Richard on the left shoulder with the spikey whip engraving deep cuts and releasing much blood. Rich-ard falls back grabbing and releasing shampoo from the open bottle onto her exposed eyes.

Richard slips up and falls down on his behind. She puts her boot heel on his neck seeking to crush it. With his last bit of strength re-maining, he wildly swings his left leg tripping her up while she was overconfident.

As she regains her footing, Richard rolls away to his right and grabs the knife from her left hand. Richard and his opponent circle each other around the shower in anticipation of a rematch, each with a weapon in hand. The masked female attempts to wrap her whip around Richard's hand carrying the laser knife. As Richard begins to drop the knife, he leans down anticipating a kick in the face, catching his opponent's foot before impact.

Richard gets the masked female on the floor and puts his foot on her neck.

"Yield," Richard said.

"Finish me while you can," the masked female said.

"Time. Richard, get dressed. This match is over," the instructor said, who appeared in the bathroom.

"Yes sir," Richard said.

The instructor looked at the masked female with disgust. "Get up," the instructor said.

"Yes sir," the masked female said.

After getting dressed and brushing his teeth, Richard heads to the cafeteria, not knowing what to expect next. Everyone is ordered to pick up the same food and no one is to eat until all have been served and seated. Some have already built up too much of an appetite that ended up overcoming them. Those who ate first started throwing up and then collapsed onto the table head first or the floor back first.

The instructors then came into the cafeteria when those who were left did not want to eat or drink anything. "You must all eat something to pass," one of the instructors said. Richard noticed some discoloration on his egg white underneath the yoke. He did not want to touch that. Something did not smell right with the bacon. He did not want to eat that. He poured the milk on the rice and the rice turned gray. That is not good. The texture on one half of the toast differs from the other. Richard eats the smoother half and nothing happens.

One of the instructors now comes to Richard saying, "Drink something now."

Only the orange juice and water are left. Both, neither, or one could be poisoned. The milk was in a glass, the water was in a cup, but the orange juice was in an unopened carton. Richard went with the orange juice and got a 'C' for his grade since his whole assessment of the breakfast took so long. Then, the lights quickly went off.

Everyone was ordered to report to Infiltration Maze (I.M.). I.M. is an underground complex under the orphanage consisting of multiple virtual reality zones and rooms. When the lights are off, the entrance doors disappear and are replaced with an illusion of a wall. In the hallway leading up to the entrance, the darkness shrouds any wanderers from seeing anyone or anything.

While up against the walls, Richard could not hear anything other than the heating system running. There is not enough time to feel the whole hallway for an opening. Richard knew that other classmates were searching for a way into I.M. Richard asked if anyone had a cigarette lighter and either some cigarettes or cigars. Enough classmates started smoking and triggered the fire alarms and sprinklers. Looking at areas where the water stopped and progressed further during the fire alarm flashes, the illusion masking the secret entrance to I.M. was unveiled. All quickly proceeded and were scolded for taking so long to get there.

Everyone is separated and must go on individual missions and deal with artificial intelligences and virtual environments that are sometimes nearly impossible to differentiate from reality. In Richard's mission, he must get inside a warehouse where a prisoner with important information is rumored to be held. Richard quickly got under a jeep as he saw a security guard coming.

This security guard goes further down the parking lot to continue his patrol runs. He whispers to another security guard. In response, this other security guard comes toward the jeep with a sniffing dog. Richard has to make a move before they reach the jeep he is under. While the security guard and his dog are still multiple vehicles away and occupied with their search, Richard crawls from underneath the jeep and makes his to other vehicles on the parking lot, eventually to the side warehouse entrance.

One guard near the entrance walks away to patrol another area while another guard remains. Richard takes this opportunity to mug the security guard near the door and uses his badge to get in. The opening of the door sounds off an alarm. Richard makes his way quickly to a bathroom and hides in one of the toilet stalls. Things calm down and two guards come in the bathroom complaining about their prisoner's huge appetite and the food they are bringing back to him.

Through sneaking past more guards, passing by openings in security cameras, and not triggering any laser trip wires, Richard follows the two guards to their destination, but most improvise to get into the room guarded by three more guards. They start playing a card game and Richard steals some of their cards making each believe the other is cheating. They start arguing and fighting while Richard sneaks into the entrance.

Richard sees the prisoner being given his food by the other two guards. The prisoner makes eye contact with Richard. When the two guards leave, they do not notice the little crack in the door, the prisoner left open for Richard.

The prisoner wearing eye glasses, a superhero logo t-shirt, jeans, and worn-out tennis shoes looks at Richard.

"Can you get me out of here?" the prisoner asked.

"Yes," Richard said.

"What do you want in return?" the prisoner asked.

"Information," Richard said.

"Deal," the prisoner said.

"Take my hand," Richard said.

The prisoner did such and found himself slowly dropping to the floor with Richard's assistance. The little tack on Richard's hand inserted a serum into the prisoner, getting him to whisper answers to Richard's questions. Richard exited from the room and warehouse with the extracted information, leaving the prisoner there, not feeling the slightest hint of conviction.

Then, reality changed and Richard saw himself walking on the sky on an invisible bridge. On the other side of the bridge leading to the city is the same masked woman that gave him a run for this money earlier.

"You again?" Richard said.

"You had your chance," the masked woman said.

Richard and this woman enter what is called Rival Mode in I.M. The only thing real is the mutual desire of both rivals to take each other down.

A laser pistol manifested within each of their reaches. The environment around them constantly changed. They went from an invisible bridge to underwater to a crowded beach to a busy construction site to a videogame arcade to a shopping mall during Christmas. Shots were fired but they only managed to graze each other in the midst of the obstacles around them. Then, they experienced a cave-in and plunged into a volcano, which blasted them into outer space. Then, a giant green alien tri-clops squid grabbed the masked woman and knocked her laser pistol away.

Richard relished this new rivalry to such an extent that he came back for the masked woman and shot the tri-clops squid in his three eyes. During this painful moment, the tri-clops squid threw the masked woman. Richard looked for her, but it was too late. She stabbed him in the back with a laser knife. The virtual session ended with the masked woman the victor.

The woman removed her mask and revealed a beautiful brown skin teenager his age with long flowing, black hair. "Richard, you should have finished me off earlier," the woman said.

"I ran out of time," Richard said.

"Remember, I am Due," Due said.

"We are due for a rematch," Richard said.

Richard was reminded of the basic lesson to not let your present opponent become your future opponent. Both passed their exams, but Due came in first place. That day, both a rivalry and professional friendship formed that would only be matched by their growing passion for each other.

WAREHOUSE

UNION

A group of hackers stumbles across a few foreign computer parts and software that lead them into discovering additional parts and software pointing towards a group of gigantic alien robots that crash landed on Earth in their shuttle centuries ago. Some of the software and hardware still function and automatically adapts to the English language.

Through reverse engineering, the hackers are able to create new hardware and software products, quickly becoming multi-millionaires. Some of the money is used for special digging excavations for more alien robotics technologies and other special R&D projects.

Within one of their warehouses, the hackers develop an innovative suite of software tools called Dark Force. It is a dominating operating system, virus, artificial intelligence, and so much more all in one. Dark Force eventually cripples and controls everything dependent upon or interfacing with networks and software.

When various government forces come against Dark Force and the hackers, the fruits of another secret project are revealed. Dark Force managed and implemented the engineering and construction of ten colossal robotic titans. Each titan has its own distinct personality, reflecting an attribute of Dark Force.

Dark Force and his titans conquer the world and are worshipped as gods. Different warehouses are set up for manufacturing and recycling titan idols, titan parts, and titan upgrades. Schools, businesses, and media are restructured to focus on the Dark Force titans' needs, wishes, and propaganda. Starting in middle school, children spend the morning in school for four hours and after a lunch break, spend the next six to eight hours working in warehouses.

Our story opens up in one such warehouse, International Recycling Technologies Warehouse 372. Walter's parents both had to work two shifts today and were not able to pick him up when he missed the school bus that normally takes him to work. He eventually found a teacher that had enough pity on him to provide a ride to work.

Walter has been late once before. He was just given a stern warning then, but realizes he will not be as lucky this time if he is late again. He rushes through the employee side door and dashes to scan his badge against the available time clock. There is no time to use the bathroom. He knows he is running late because he sees no one in the smoke room as he passes by. He has to make it to his workstation before the bell. No one is happy here. Some are silent while others are trying to joke around to keep their sanity. For his sake, Walter just gets to his workstation before the bell.

"That girl kept you late after school again, Walter?" Maury said.

"Not today. Physical Ed went over," Walter said.

"I bet. You got a real workout today," Maury said.

"Don't you ever stop, Maury?" Walter said.

"Do you?" Maury said.

"You two better keep up and not put all this work on me!" Old Rachel said.

"Will do," Walter said.

Walter thought, of all the conveyors to receive recyclable part from and sort, why did his workstation have to be around Maury, who is always making mischievous suggestions and off-color jokes?

Walter takes a rusted component to remove some reusable chips, but is pricked in his finger by an unexpected sharp protrusion at the end of it. Walter's hand then trembles uncontrollably. Then, his arm goes numb not being able to move it.

"You alright, Walter?" Maury said.

"A bad case of tendonitis," Walter said.

"Shake it off man," Maury said.

Walter takes his working hand and puts a band aid over his finger and takes another Tylenol for pain. Then, he can move his arm again, while feeling a slight sensation in his neck. Old Rachel complains again about Walter needing to keep up.

There are no more strange incidents throughout the rest of the workday and Walter uses his voucher card to use the shuttle taking him and others home. When he arrives, Walter notices that his parents still have not made it home yet. Dinner is provided to the working minors at work during the shift. Walter makes it upstairs to his bedroom and then collapses on the bed.

"Do you always go to bed this early?" an unknown female voice said.

"Who is there?" Walter said. Walter got up to reach for his baseball bat.

"That will not be necessary," the unknown female voice said.

"Where are you? Show yourself!" Walter said.

"I am in your head, hot stuff," the unknown female voice said.

"I am going to get you," Walter said.

"Too late. I already got you," the unknown female voice said.

Walter looked around, but still could not find anyone.

"Go to the mirror," the unknown female voice said.

"I am not playing your game," Walter said.

"Then open your right sleeve and you will see that this is no game honey," the unknown female voice said.

Walter notices a tattoo resembling an orange monarch butterfly on his right arm. "How did you do this to me?" Walter said.

"We are engaged lover," the unknown female voice said.

"What's going on here?" Walter said.

"I am going to rock your world, Walter," the unknown female voice said.

"Who are you and what do you want?" Walter said.

"Wortel. I want you," Wortel said.

"The lack of sleep is really getting to me," Walter said.

"Help me defeat Dark Force and you will get all of the rest you ever wanted and much more," Wortel said.

"I am helping myself go to asleep, and not talking to you anymore. I am not losing it all today," Walter said.

"Please look in the mirror again," Wortel said.

Walter, who is desperately tired, just looks into the mirror to stop this inner nagging. What he sees is unrecognizable. He does not see himself in the mirror anymore. What he sees instead is someone taller in some form of an external bio-organic body suit that looks completely alien. "Is this you?" Walter said.

"No, I am all over you and in you at the same time. For better or worse, we are one," Wortel said.

"Now, you're saying, we're married?" Walter said.

"We might as well. I am not going anywhere. Do you want a test drive?" Wortel said.

"I want to be my old self again!" Walter said.

"You cannot be that person ever again," Wortel said.

"How can you do this to me?" Walter said.

"Because I love you," Wortel said.

"I am a monster!" Walter said.

"No, you're not," Wortel said.

The bio-organic body suit disappears and Walter looks like his old self again. "Thank you, Wortel," Walter said.

"Don't thank me yet. Our honey moon is almost over. We have a mission coming soon," Wortel said.

"Yes. I am on Mission Z," Walter said. He fell back into his bed like a triple knock-out.

Walter now sees himself in a park with plenty of sunshine and flowers. There are other children playing and laughing. The air has never felt and the water has never looked this clean before. There is much laughter and joy everywhere. Walter notices a beautiful bare-footed female teenager wearing a multicolored flower dress sitting on a park bench feeding the birds. Her yellow skin was as radiant as a summer sun and her alluring waist length red hair could easily light a passionate admirer's fire. A mesmerized Walter approaches this young lady.

"Hello Walter," the young lady with the flower dress said.

"Wortel, is that you?" Walter said.

"Yes, it is handsome," Wortel said.

Walter could see the power surging in Wortel's eyes.

"Walter, please sit beside me," Wortel said.

"Sure," Walter said.

The birds near Wortel fly away.

"This is who I am Walter. You normally cannot see me because I am microscopic in size. When you stuck yourself with that rusted component, I entered inside you and travelled through your hand to your arm and eventually made my way to your brain," Wortel said.

"Why me?" Walter said.

"My father is a human and he chose you. We are the Cocci. A Coccus reproduces by either a male Coccus bonding with a female host or a female Coccus bonding with a male host. The bio-organic body suit that the host wears eventually produces eggs giving birth to new Cocci who then enter a world's atmosphere finding new hosts. We keep a telepathic link with our parents and host. We can also communicate with nearby Cocci. Right now, we are engaged. The tattoo on your arm is a symbol of our engagement. Once we pass the engagement period with my parents' approval, our union will be permanent. We will then be enabled to reproduce. While you are asleep, we can see each other and share special moments. I will forever be in your dreams," Wortel said.

Walter was speechless.

"You are cute when you look confused Walter," Wortel said.

"Wortel, you are the girl of my dreams," Walter said.

"Come closer Walter," Wortel said. Wortel kissed Walter.

Walter wakes up and sees himself flying in his bio-organic body suit with butterfly wings. There are other people flying in their bio-organic body suits with him. They are approaching a junior titan. Dark Force is now producing smaller titan robots to carry out the will of the larger original titans. This junior titan is still a giant.

"Wortel, are we still dreaming?" Walter said.

"My parents summoned us for our first mission together. This is as real as it gets. I will guide you every step of the way," Wortel said.

Walter noticed one of his teammates climbing on the junior titan's back, with another on the leg, and one more shooting at his eyes.

"Two of your teammates are looking for an infiltration point. Dark Force always places an infiltration point on a junior titan to ensure one does not get out of line. Let's help them find it," Wortel said.

Walter notices an anomaly on the back of the junior titan's head. "Walter, I will help you fire some stinger blasts on that spot. We will have to move inside the titan quickly, because once an infiltration point has been discovered, it will seal and move to a different area of the body," Wortel said.

"Let's do this," Walter said. Walter fires the stinger blasts from his body suit and gets inside the junior titan's head through the penetrated infiltration point, which quickly seals. "What now?" Walter said.

"We do not have far to travel. Let's destroy his mind," Wortel said.

Travelling inside the junior titan's body was like travelling through a living, evolving factory, combined with multiple power plants and computer servers. All were protected by robotic bats, worms, bats, drones, and smaller ships of all shapes and sizes. "Let's hurry, Walter! Go straight up and do not stop for anything! We are outgunned and outmanned. I will try to cover us with some vapor bombs," Wortel said.

With an entourage behind them, they reached a gigantic encased vial. Some additional appendages extend from Walter's body suit's hands and melts the encasing. Then something poisonous emits from the extra appendages and what was in the vial dissipates. The pursuing entourage plunges to their doom.

"Walter, this titan is going to self-destruct soon. We have to get out of here!" Wortel said.

"How?" Walter said.

"There must be another opening somewhere. Try the eyes!" Wortel said. Wortel was right on target.

When Walter made it out, he was welcomed to the resistance group known as Anti-Titan (A.T.) by his new teammates. Then, as Walter was making his way back home, he said to Wortel, "Let's work things out between us."

"I will love that very much, Walter. We are better together as one than two," Wortel said.

We know that it takes more than defeating a basic junior titan to stop Dark Force. The engagement between Walter and Wortel has just begun and so has their involvement in the war against Dark Force. They are not alone.

Relationships will have varying origins, but when two can become one, such a bond is not easily broken. There is someone sent into this world to become one with you. It is our job to find this person or be found by this person. When the time comes for such a unification, do not let anyone or anything divide you.

THE UNDERGROUND CITY

There comes a time in your life when you simply need to start over and leave the past behind. Depending upon how you respond, yesterday's troubles can either propel you into greater triumphs or lead you into one final tragedy. The present is one of the greatest gifts that you have today. What will you do with it?

Tomorrow cannot wait. Aarush has to make a run for it tonight. This twelve-year-old has made it through multiple lifetimes of pain, loneliness, and abuse. His current pursuer has given him more punishment than he can endure. If he can just leave the sticks, and make it to the city that is not too far passed the one-car length old town bridge, just maybe he can find a new opportunity there.

Aarush catches his breath at the old town bridge. Then, trouble pulls up behind him to suffocate what hope remains.

"Little A, get your butt back in this car now!" a middle-aged man said.

"I am not going with you," Aarush said.

"You don't talk to your old man like that," the middle age man said.

"You are not my father, just a man collecting a check. Man, I will jump before I go back with you!" Aarush said.

"You think you're a man now?" Aarush's foster father said.

By this time, Aarush's foster father was out of the car, limping along to Aarush.

"You want to be a man; I will treat you like a man," Aarush's foster father said.

"At least I would be a man instead of a monster," Aarush said.

Aarush's foster father smacks Aarush in the face like he is a fly being smashed by a flyswatter. Aarush kicks his foster father in the right leg that he previously stabbed him with to escape from the car earlier. That does not even buy Aarush enough time to run away, as the man he describes as a monster, lunges on him, ripping his shirt to shreds, proceeding to pull his pants down.

"You will not do this to me again," Aarush said.

Enraged, the monster of a man smashes Aarush's face against the road side of the bridge multiple times. He then lifts the battered Aarush up.

"You will not be needing this anymore either," Aarush's foster father said. He took out the knife that Aarush stabbed him with and then stabbed Aarush in the chest with it.

"God will avenge me," Aarush said.

"Go tell him, "Hi.", for me," Aarush's foster father said. He threw Aarush over the side of the bridge.

Aarush did not rise up again. Only blood did. Thinking his work has been done, the monster of the man heads home knowing that his wife will not question him. She has turned a blind eye to all that he has done over the years because of the money he brings to the table. A few foster children are just another hustle. No one is going to miss another black child lost in the system.

Aarush then wakes up, finding himself on a hospital bed connected to various machines and tubes. The lights are off, but he sees a window with water on the outside, implying that this hospital is either part of an aquarium or is literally underwater. Then, the hospital room door opens.

In the darkness, the people that come in and surround him appear to be something other than human. They speak in languages he does not understand. The lights come on and all appear to be human, with him understanding what is being spoken.

"Good, you are finally awake," one of the doctors said.

Aarush then blacks out, submitting to a greater force.

Aarush feels no more pain and is floating. He actually sees the doctors and staff examining his body still tied to the machines and tubes. Aarush feels the urge to draw closer to the window. Aarush walks through the window. Even while walking underwater, Aarush can breathe and does not feel damp at all. He can see all and does not have any heaviness. All of the fishes and plants are unfamiliar to him. They do not look like anything of this world, if he is still on Earth. Even though, what he sees is alien to him, the different combinations of shapes, sizes, colors, are still very beautiful. The water color fluctuates between blue and purple.

Aarush tries to look for the window leading to the hospital room where his body resides, but cannot find his way back. A large animal resembling a whale mixed with other things, heads towards Aarush, but goes right through him. Aarush starts to fully comprehend that he may not make it back to his body. Aarush starts to fear that it could be too late for him and he is already dead. In spite of all the beauty around him, Aarush is nothing more than a ghost trying to interact with an underwater Eden that will not connect with him. Aarush is summoned upward by an unknown force into a mountain.

Inside the mountain, Aarush sees an underground metropolis unlike any other. Unlike the sea life, everyone in the city appears to be of Earth, but notices all races and cultures are represented, in harmony with each other. There is no respect of persons, with everyone being treated as equals. Culture transcends race, but the unique contributions of each culture are highly valued.

Everything in this city is clean and feels new. Even though the city is underground, the light that somehow makes it down overpowers the darkness. There is more light here than meets the eye. No appearance of slums or poverty are present. There is prosperity for everyone everywhere.

Being human, Aarush tries to reach out to the other people around him. No matter how hard he tries to communicate with those around him, no one appears to see or hear him. People actually walk right through him as if he does not exist. Then suddenly, Aarush hears a voice saying, "Run!"

There are silent people in black hoods that walk towards Aarush. Even though he feels like a ghost, he does not want to take a chance with these strangers, so he runs. No one else in the city appears to notice the silent people in black hoods. Everywhere Aarush hides, every building he goes through, and every height he ascends or descends, the silent people in black hoods are there.

Aarush makes it to a temple, looking for hope there. No help is to be found while he is surrounded by the forces of darkness. The silent people with the black hoods have formed a circle around Aarush and each start pulling out their knives. This circle of death closes in around Aarush as paralysis comes upon him.

"Be gone!" an older African female said.

All of the silent people with black hoods disappear as puffs of smoke.

"Thank you," Aarush said.

"Are you truly grateful young man?" the older African female said.

"Yes Ma'am," Aarush said.

"What did you think of the city?" the older African female said.

"It was the most beautiful city I have ever seen in my life. I wish I could live there," Aarush said.

"Do you really?" the older African female said.

"Was that city Heaven, and I died? Did those people in black-hoods try to drag me down to Hell?" Aarush said.

"Young man, do you claim life or death?" the older African female asked.

"Life," Aarush responded.

"Do you seek love or hunger for hatred?" the older African female asked.

"Love," Aarush responded.

"Is their peace or war in your heart?" the older African female asked.

"Peace," Aarush responded.

"What do you value more, the past or the future?" the older African female asked.

"Definitely, the future," Aarush responded.

"What is your loyalty to, mankind or goodness?" the older African female asked.

"Goodness, because God knows all," Aarush responded.

"Young man, can a man become God?" the older African female asked.

"No, but we can still become great through Him," Aarush responded.

"Young man, you are a very curious one indeed. Let us put you to the test," the older African female said.

"Test?" Aarush said.

"Why, of course. Off you go," the older African female said. Then, Aarush himself disappears like a puff of smoke.

Aarush is back in a familiar place. He has returned to what some would call home. The rooms in the house themselves are clean, but there is much filth here. The air smells pure, but corruption has set in the atmosphere. The front door is being unlocked. Aarush goes to the kitchen.

Aarush's foster parents come inside with Aarush's younger foster brother and another young man who appears to be similar in age as Aarush. They all have grocery bags in their hands. Aarush's younger foster brother accidentally drops the eggs and breaks them. His foster father responds by slapping the back of his neck like a fly. The young man fell to the ground and did not respond. Neither did his foster mother. Aarush's replacement was in shock.

"That is enough!" Aarush said.

"It can't be!" Aarush's foster father said.

"Yes, it is!" Aarush said.

"Honey, we missed you!" Aarush's foster mother said. Out of fear, Aarush's foster mother came running up to Aarush to hug him, but then found herself going through him.

"You are a ghost! Stay away from us!" Aarush's foster father said.

"Stay away from them!" Aarush said. Aarush's rage manifested fire in the house. "You belong in Hell with the other monsters!" Aarush said.

"No, I did not mean to kill you! I am so sorry!" Aarush's foster father said.

The fire grew and Aarush walked closer to the monster that caused him so much pain. As he looked at him, he remembered his conversation with the older African woman. He realizes that he answered her questions correctly, but he must now past the test and move forward.

"You are not worth it," Aarush said. Then mist manifested swallowing the fire.

"I love you honey," Aarush's foster mother said.

"You did nothing to help us when he abused us. You are just as bad as him, but I forgive you. I am going to a better place now," Aarush said. Aarush looked upon his younger foster brother and he started to recover. "Farewell, little brother," Aarush said.

"Aarush?" Aarush's younger foster brother said. By that time, Aarush already disappeared.

"He is a perfect match," a voice said.

Aarush wakes up in his body and is greeted by doctors, nurses, and others welcoming him to his new home.

"Welcome to Anu," one of the doctors said. Then a glowing couple with inviting smiles come closer to Aarush.

"Son, regardless of where you have been, you have a home with us now. We are the Godfreys. What is your name?" the Godfreys asked.

"Aarush," Aarush said.

"Aarush, you are a Godfrey now and a miracle child. The doctors told us about your body's full recovery. You just had to wake up and now you are," the Godfreys said.

For the first time in quite some time, Aarush smiles. "Thank you," Aarush said.

No matter where you are in life, there is a higher place to ascend to and a greater ideal to uphold. Never deny what you are, but make sure what you are matches up with who you are. Do not forsake your future by refusing to forgive. In the present, no longer excuse or just cope with the abuses of the past. There is a better place to go to, but the journey progresses on how we respond. How will you respond to your opportunity when it comes?

THE NEW KID

Three generations ago, A meteor of extraterrestrial origin came towards the Earth and scattered into multiple fragments when it exploded upon reaching Earth's atmosphere. The fragments of the meteor came to be known as X11. The first "one" represents its universal alien element properties. The second "one" represents the unique effect X11 has on the person that comes into contact with it and absorbs it power.

Ultimately, this led to an age of superheroes and supervillains, with the superheroes being the victors. What humanity did not realize was that all were true losers. X11 led to mental breakdowns, instability, and corruption among both superheroes and supervillains. Even during their metamorphoses, arch foes would not work together, despite their new natures. This led to one final battle where many were killed, those who had powers and those who did not.

The surviving superheroes felt some remorse and formed one super team, conquering the rest of the inhabitable world in an attempt to restore order under a totalitarian government ruled by them. To keep total control, the super team implemented a device that reached across the world, scrambling people's ability to read and write. The only humans immune to this were those who resided in the domed cities created by the government as a defense against the super beings. No one can enter or leave the domed cities.

Unfortunately, some of the super team's rogues' gallery also hide out in these domed cities, causing havoc. The government's offense against the super beings was the Battle Other Terrorists (B.O.T.) program. Dr. Sullivan Zimmerman was the founder of this program and had thirteen prototypes. Each prototype was part human, part machine cyborg with the ability to replicate the powers and abilities of the super beings, and evolve their powers and abilities automatically with their additional experiences. Unfortunately, a group of supervillain mercenaries attacked and destroyed the underground lab with a cave in. There were no known survivors. The status of the prototypes remains a mystery until this very day.

How much of a cyborg is a man? Is it the part that dreams or has dreams? What should be considered ground truth, programmed protocols or memory fragments that give more questions than answers? Has the soul become just as artificial as the shell that houses him? Is his spirit still in control of this shell or held prisoner, along with the rest of his soul? Did his power truly come from man or someone or something else much greater?

In the midst of the rubble, a living soul rises. This rubble was once a state-of-the-art laboratory to help preserve the future of mankind, but has now become another crypt, and perhaps the nail in the coffin for man. The living soul sees pain and destruction all around him, but feels nothing. Everything in this cave just goes through him. It is like he is nothing more than a disembodied spirit, but is then reminded of a higher calling, when his rebooted systems activate a holographic message.

A hologram of Dr. Sullivan Zimmerman appears. "Son, they are coming here soon. You are what is left of my son and my hope for mankind. I will tend to the others, but you are my first priority, because you are my son. I am activating your ghost state so that you will survive and awaken when mankind needs you the most. If you are seeing this message, that time is now. You are my son, Jay Zimmerman, but also B-12, the thirteenth prototype. There are no more superheroes now, only supervillains. I have given you a special program nicknamed The Bible Program to depower supervillains and restore a person's ability to read and write. When you reach the right maturity, you will learn the code word to access it and how to administer it. Also, through your experiences, your mind, state, and power abilities shall evolve and multiply. Restore mankind to greatness my son. I love you and let no one discourage or stop you from fulfilling your God given purpose. You will hear from me again at the destined time," Dr. Zimmerman said. Then, he is gone.

A renewed, repurposed Jay Zimmerman first goes to search for any others in the rubble, but finds no one alive. There are many skeletons, bloodshed, and crushed dreams to go around. In the midst of all of this wreckage, there are no traces of the twelve prototypes before him. His brethren are nowhere to be found. Perhaps, there is some hope for them. There is nothing else left for Jay Zimmerman here. He ascends in his ghost state to begin his purpose and perhaps some other things as well. He will have to settle for being B-12 for now.

B-12 arrives in a parking garage filled with cars, but isolated at this time. It is during these isolated moments, the biggest bullies come out to claim what belongs to others and usurp their authority over human decency. Two potential victims have just been spotted by B-12.

"This mall is under my protection. You were warned to pay my fee for safe passage each month. Now you will pay the price!" a person in gigantic red knight armor said.

"We were just trying to get some supplies. Red Knight, do you have a heart within that armor?" a brown skinned teenage female with shoulder length hair replied.

"I will have yours instead," Red Knight said.

Then, bullet shots were fired near Red Knight's eyes.

"Run Aisha!" Aisha's brown-haired male companion said.

As the teenage duo attempts to flee, Red Knight chuckles. He casts a net upon them that trips the couple up. "Now, prepare yourselves," Red Knight said.

"Prepare yourself for a new challenger, Red Knight," B-12 said.

"Who dares?" Red Knight said.

"B-12 does," B-12 said.

"This will be fun," Red Knight said. Red Knight comes charging at B-12 and swings his sword. The sword goes right through B-12.

"What?" Red Knight said.

B-12 in his ghost state charges through Red Knight. This causes Red Knight's armor to malfunction. Caught off guard once again, Red Knight staggers out of the parking garage.

"Thank you for saving us!" Aisha said.

"You're welcome. I am B-12," B-12 said.

"Nice to meet you B-12. I'm Aisha and this is Ted," Aisha said.

"Yes, thank you again. We should go," Ted said.

"You're not from around here, are you B-12?" Aisha said.

"I don't know. Dr. Zimmerman sent me," B-12 said.

"Dr. Zimmerman, you said?" Ted said.

"Yes," B-12 said.

"Do you mind having dinner with us?" Ted said.

"That is a great idea, Ted! What do you say, B-12?" Aisha said.

"Why would you invite a ghost to dinner?" B-12 said.

"Let's figure this out B-12. It is the least we could do since you helped us," Ted said.

"I'll give it a try," B-12 said.

B-12 in his ghost state tries to keep up with Ted's van, on the inside, while it is moving. The equipment and junk inside the back of this van remind him of a mad scientist enamored with robotics. As they are driving out of the city to a rural location, they are still surrounded by a clear, all-encompassing dome that follows them everywhere.

"Why are we inside a dome?" B-12 said.

"This is the only thing keeping our brains from being scrambled like most people. Without it, we will not be able to read and write," Ted said.

"We can still travel between cities and get other things done through the underground subway network that we have. Anyone with X11 is not allowed to break through or out of the dome through a programmed genetic scanner barrier," Aisha said.

"What about a ghost?" B-12 said.

"Good question," Aisha said.

"You are not going to stay a ghost," Ted said.

"How so?" B-12 said.

"Let's get to the house first," Ted said.

They finally made it to a large white house in the woods, which has aged, but is still maintained well. Ted gets out a remote. After he pushes a button, an electrical barrier surrounding the house is removed, but the dome around them remains. The van then drives down a ramp leading to a garage that is attached to the house at the basement level. B-12 helps Ted and Aisha get their stuff in.

Ted's basement reminded B-12 of a scaled down B.O.T. program laboratory.

"What exactly are you doing here Ted?" B-12 said.

"I am continuing my father's work. I hope to use robotics to make things better in this city and protect us from the super villains," Ted said.

"Have you seen others like me?" B-12 said.

"You are the first and maybe the last," Ted said.

"So be it," B-12 said.

"Ted, before we eat, weren't you going to help B-12?" Aisha said.

"Yes. B-12, rapidly increase the heat settings in your systems and you should eventually become solid again," Ted said.

Ted was right and B-12 became solid again.

"I feel alive once again! Thank you, Ted!" B-12 said.

"Catch," Aisha said.

B-12 caught the bottle.

"That is not all. Rapidly increase the cooling settings in your system and you will be in the ghost state again," Ted said.

B-12 dropped the water bottle. "Sorry Aisha," B-12 said. He quickly solidified and picked up the water bottle to hand back to Aisha. She then handed B-12 a penny.

"Penny for your thoughts?" Aisha said.

"B-12, hold that penny in your hand. With just a thought, you can absorb some of the properties from a metallic object, even as small as a penny, and transform into a metal state. Give it a try," Ted said.

B-12 did and he reached a metal state from absorbing some of the metallic properties from the penny. To be free of the metal state, B-12 had to first transform into the ghost state.

"One more thing, B-12. Something can trigger a transformation into an energy state. I am not sure how to bring about this transformation," Ted said.

"I thank you for teaching me these things Ted, but how do you know all of this? Where did you get all of this equipment from?" B-12 said. Then, the lights went off.

"Ted, the generator power is not even coming on!" Aisha said.

"Let's go upstairs," Ted said. Ted and Aisha turn on their flash lights and when they reach upstairs, there is only complete darkness everywhere.

"I have not seen it this bad before," Aisha said.

"They are redirecting all back-up generator power to just keep the dome going," Ted said.

"Look at how the dome is no longer transparent. The dome is now solid black," B-12 said.

"If our power situation does not improve soon, more supervillains may come in. Even worse, our brains could become scrambled and we lose our abilities to read and write," Ted said.

"That is not going to happen Ted! B-12?" Aisha said.

"I will find the one place that still has power. Will both of you be alright here?" B-12 said.

"We have guns and some laser pistols that still work. Please, hurry though and be careful yourself. There are monsters in the woods at night. Take this micro battery powered walkie talkie," Ted said.

"We'll be in touch," B-12 said.

B-12 stealthily makes his way through the darkness to his destination. He notices one powerplant surround by police and other armed forces. There is a forced lightning storm preventing anyone from entering. B-12 reaches out to Ted through the micro walkie talkie.

"Ted, are you there?" B-12 said.

"Yes, B-12. Go ahead," Ted said. "Whoever has taken over the Douglas Powerplant prevents anyone from getting in by striking all visible targets with some form of continuous lightening blasts all over the perimeter," B-12 said.

"True, but that will not work against a ghost," Ted said.

"That is a good one Ted. Thanks," B-12 said. B-12 tried to forget being a ghost, but he has no choice in becoming one again.

While everyone is distracted, B-12 in his ghost state slips through. Once inside, he is greeted by a group with body protection coveralls. They are all amazed how their weapons, physical attacks, and other projectiles go right through B-12. Eventually, B-12 is dismissed as a literal ghost and everyone B-12 approaches runs for it. Finally, he reaches the mastermind behind this operation.

"So, you are the ghost everyone is making a fuss about?" the mastermind said.

"I am that and much more," B-12 said.

"What do you want, ghost?" the mastermind said.

"Who are you and why are you doing this?" B-12 said.

"I am Trip. I need this power to get out of here and take on the super team, Republic of Heroes, who have trapped us all," Trip said.

"What about the people here? Without power for their dome, their brains will become scrambled like so many others. They will lose their abilities to read and write," B-12 said.

"That is their problem. Being trapped in this dome by those super hypocrites is no life at all," Trip said.

"I cannot let you continue doing this," B-12 said.

"Just what are you going to do about it?" Trip said.

"Do this!" B-12 said. He comes charging at Trip in his ghost form and much to his chagrin, this has no effect on Trip.

"Brother, you must be tripping," Trip said. Trip starts to leave. B-12 lands in front of the exit.

"I will just go through you," Trip said.

Then, a solidified B-12 punches Trip in the face.

"It is going to take more than that," Trip said.

"I got more than enough to share," B-12 said.

"But will you be able to put yourself back together again?" Trip said.

"Let's see," B-12 said. "I will light you up," Trip said. Trip's power has been greatly amplified from absorbing so much electricity. He unleashes a barrage of electric blasts that burn B-12 to a crisp. "That was simple. What was that fool thinking?" Trip said.

"I guess you are tripping, brother," B-12 said. This time, B-12 is different. He is in an energy state resembling a fiery sun.

"So, the ghost has returned," Trip said.

"It is not that simple," B-12 said.

What follows next is a clash between what seems like the sun and lightning. "We keep fighting like this, we are going to blow up this entire city," B-12 said.

"You are nothing but practice for the main event," Trip said. Their fight takes them near the water storage area. B-12 fires at the massive storage, allowing both of them to be engulfed in this tsunami of water.

There were two, but now there is only one. B-12 could not accumulate enough cooling internally to change back into his ghost state and remained in his energy state. Still, even in his weakened state, he rises. Trip is not so lucky. B-12's fortunes are still in question as the authorities arrive.

"Boy, am I glad to see you. I stopped Trip for you," B-12 said. The police said nothing and started firing at B-12.

"Wait! I stopped the bad guy for you! Stop shooting! My hands are up!" B-12 said.

"Your kind is all the same!" one police officer said. They keep firing at B-12 who melts their bullets in his energy state. B-12 runs away and eventually musters enough strength to leave the building in his ghost state.

The lights come back on throughout the city, but the people are blinded with more fear and hatred than ever when they see B-12 on the streets.

"Another X11 monster! He must have caused this! Let's get him!" some people in the crowd said. A mob starts to chase B-12 in his ghost state.

"Come down here," a voice said. B-12 starts sinking deeper underground into the sewers.

B-12 is greeted by a white and green man frog with yellow webbed hands and eyes.

"Greetings, friend. You must be another X11 monster like me. Call me M.F.," M.F. said.

"M.F., what is X11?" B-12 said.

"What planet are you from?" M.F. said.

"Good question," B-12 said.

"Only special people hear my telepathic summons. You must be one of us. Come with me," M.F. said.

"Can you tell me how to get to Southern Woods?" B-12 said.

"There is nothing for you there," M.F. said.

"That is for me to decide," B-12 said.

"You have latent mental powers. I will now activate them for you to teach you a lesson," M.F. said.

B-12 returned to his solid state and punched M.F. with an electrically charged punched that shocked him.

"You will definitely make an interesting addition to my army, but first you must learn your lesson," M.F. said.

Before B-12 can strike again, M.F.'s telepathic powers overwhelm him. "Your mental powers have now been activated. You now see the truth for yourself and will then beg to join me. You now know where to find me," M.F. said as he walked away.

Having telepathic powers activated without the proper training and psychic shielding can overcome the average person, leading to a mental breakdown of epic proportions. B-12 can now hear the hateful and fearful thoughts of those above him. He hears the little things and meatier matters. He hears that Trip is still alive but requiring medical attention. He hears more thoughts than he can process.

With what is left of his own thoughts, B-12 telepathically reaches out to Ted and Aisha, and finds them.

"Where are you B-12?" Ted said.

"We really need your help B-12," Aisha said.

"I will be right there. Keep thinking about me and guide me back to you," B-12 said.

Once again, a living soul rises above the rubble to continue on the pursuit of his purpose. This time, the ghost travels much faster.

When B-12 arrives, there is a group of looters in scarecrow masks invading Ted's house. The ghost of B-12 puts them into flight, adding more lore to the mystery of Southern Woods.

"Thank you, B-12," Aisha said.

"Yeah, I thought we were goners," Ted said.

"I was almost added to that list," B-12 said.

"I see that you have grown already," Ted said.

"Let's have that long delayed dinner," Aisha said.

"What do you feed someone like me?" B-12 said.

"The part of you that is human will figure that out," Aisha said.

"You are more human than what you think," Ted said.

One finds a new family, another tries to rectify the sins of his family, and one more still does not know what has happened to her family. Stay tuned.

LOVE AT FIRST SIGHT

A generation from now, commercial space travel between the Earth and the Moon becomes widespread, but only affordable for the richest of the Earth's population. Several countries form alliances to compete for property on the moon. To mitigate the escalating resulting conflicts, all military stations and research facilities are consolidated into joint international collaborations for about a quarter of the Moon. A little less than a quarter of the Moon still remains as undeveloped neutral territory, considered quite dangerous.

Over half of the moon has been converted into the universe's largest collection of amusement parks and resorts. Usually, it is only the wealthy or elite that can enjoy this luxurious, once in a lifetime experience. There is no place on Earth like this. There is no place like Aylin.

Quarterly, all expenses paid vacation sweepstakes to Aylin are offered. In this year, the Blakeleys finally have their season. This middle class African American family wins a month-long vacation to the moon where they will spend all of their time at Aylin. International Monolith (I.M.), the Moon's joint international military and research complex, is off limits to visitors unless invited. It is highly recommended for tourists to stay away from the undeveloped areas known as the Forbidden Zones. There are always questionable entrepreneurs offering tourists access to these zones at cut-rate prices. It is rumored that even a few people manage to live in the Forbidden Zones.

Travel between Earth and the Moon can now be completed within twenty-four hours. For the Blakeleys, every hour of the journey is an experience. Little do they know, how pivotal of a role the destination will play with their destinies, especially of the thirteen-year-old Corey Blakeley. Lift-off feels like a reversed rollercoaster going upward instead of downwards. Then, when things calm down, they and the other passengers are released from their belts and allowed to float around the space ship. The sight of seeing Earth from space for themselves is priceless, but overwhelming. They are awed by the size of Earth.

Also, space food has come a long way, being transformed into gourmet food with its own unique taste. This space gourmet food is served every hour. There are many entertainment venues made available throughout this commercial shuttle for all to enjoy in safety. Space travel to the Moon has been perfected, but the evolution of mankind has failed to keep pace with this technical revolution. Science can give one a better life, but it does not necessary guarantee making one a better person. Other factors still need to take center stage.

"Look Corey! The moon is welcoming us!" Kisa said.

"Yes, it is, Kisa," Corey said. That is the thing he likes most about his little ten-year old sister. She gets great joy out of the little things, but it is not every day a person sees "Welcome!" lit on the Moon.

"Corey and Kisa, we will be docking at the space station soon. Make sure you have everything," Mr. Blakeley said.

"Everyone, we have to get our belts back on soon too," Mrs. Blakeley said.

"Yes, Mom and Dad," Corey and Kisa said.

The space station is crowded, but not congested. There is much automation to keep things going. The luggage that shrank was fired back to full size. There is a lunar train to take everyone to low air transportation. On the Moon, people fly low altitude compact spacecrafts instead of ground vehicles. Before getting a craft pilot, the Blakeleys enjoy the path of the lunar train seeing many amusements, sights, and lights from afar throughout the Moon from their vantage point. The Blakeleys soak in every moment before their stop beckons.

Upon departing the lunar train, a floating robotic bell boy platform carrying their luggage follows them. They are then greeted by a silver robotic craft pilot.

"Welcome to Aylin, Blakeleys. There is no place like Aylin," the silver robotic craft pilot said.

"Thank you. There certainly isn't," Mr. Blakeley said.

The robotic bell boy platform loaded the Blakeleys' luggage into the green and silver compact spacecraft.

"Where would you like to go Mr. Blakeley?" the silver robotic craft pilot said.

"The Providence Tower," Mr. Blakely said.

"All systems go," the silver robotic craft pilot said. The compact spacecraft took off vertically and then moved within what is considered the normal traffic pattern.

"There is so much to do here, Corey. Where do we start?" Kisa said.

"How about dinner?" Corey said.

"How can you still be hungry?" Kisa said.

"You would be surprised," Corey said.

"We had a full day getting here. Let's take it easy at The Providence Tower this evening. We can start exploring tomorrow," Mrs. Blakeley said.

"Alright, Mom," Kisa said.

"Dinner it is then," Corey said.

The next morning on the moon, sunrise comes suddenly. There is no twilight from the rising of the sun, but the sun does not rise alone. Stars in the sun's vicinity rise along with it. Even with this entourage, there is always darkness. The sky remains black. There is still one shining moment the Blakeleys will not forget. Waking up early this morning to see the Earth is priceless.

As a part of their all-expenses paid trip, the Blakeleys are given a daily budget by their sponsor. Even then, this budget is quite generous, allowing them to splurge. Kisa is quite fond of the chocolate chip moon shaped waffles. Corey enjoys the enlarged double fried sunny side up eggs. Their parents enjoy the uniquely seasoned imported pork and pastries. The Blakeleys decide to go to Crescent Amusement Park first, taking another low altitude compact spacecraft to get there.

Crescent Amusement Park has a sign stating, "The Moon Rises. Rise with It."

"Corey and Kisa, this park is huge. Let's stay close to each other," Mr. Blakeley said.

"We will have fun, but let's be careful," Mrs. Blakeley said.

"Sure, Mom," Corey said.

"Wow, look at all of the lights and fireworks as we come in!" Kisa said.

Corey notices that Kisa loves changing the subject when she thinks the conversation is not going to turn her way.

The Blakeleys enter a platform after the entrance of Crescent Amusement Park. A voice in the intercom shouts, "Time to rise!" The platform then propels the Blakeleys up several stories to the amusement park's main area. There are more lights here than the largest of Earth's casinos. In Crescent Amusement Park, there is more than enough light to overshadow the darkness. There are illuminating white light orbs following everyone around the park as well. Little does everyone know that the forces of darkness never give up, always waiting for that new opportunity, an opening.

There are two classic lunar rovers serving as decoration in the main amusement park hub. All of a sudden, that which was only background props takes center stage. The two classic lunar rovers come to life driving into the crowd. Everyone scatters as sheep fleeing a pack of ravenous wolves that have revealed their true nature. Corey's parents are able to grab Kisa in time. Corey tries to stay close to them, but sees an Asian girl, who looks about his age with a purple blouse and skirt, about to be trampled by the crowd. Corey stops pursuing his family to help a stranger rise up. Then, a hovering park robot picks them both up and drops them off on a park lunar train taking them to the other side of Crescent Amusement Park. Things eventually calm down, and both Corey and the female stranger exit the train together.

"Thank you for saving me. What is your name?" the female stranger in purple said.

"Corey," Corey said.

"Is that all?" the female stranger in purple said.

"Corey Blakely," Corey said.

"That is better. My parents named me Amaya Watanabe. I prefer to just go by Amaya," Amaya said.

"Are you related to anyone from The Japanese Watanabe Corporation?" Corey said.

"Let's not talk about that Corey," Amaya said.

"I will help you get back to your family," Corey said.

"Let's take our time," Amaya said. They might as well when they find out they both cannot get a signal from their lunar phones.

"We might as well make the most of this time as we make it back to the other side of the park," Corey said.

"That is more like it, Corey," Amaya said.

There appears to be much to like about Amaya. The purple outfit Amaya wears matches up with the corporate royalty she is raised in. Her long, luscious black hair down to her waist underscores her princess status. Her purple eclipse ear rings further bait him. She has painted her nails purple to match her outfit. Corey will not be surprised if her toe nails are painted with a matching color. Her perfume smells of wealth. The make-up she wears only accentuates the beauty already there, not covering anything up. Where ever Amaya wants to go, he will gladly follow her.

"What would you like to do, Amaya?" Corey said.

"Since, we are on this side, I would like for us to go on the Crash-Landing rollercoaster, but can you handle this?" Amaya said.

"Yes, I can," Corey said, while looking at Amaya.

Be strong Corey. Corey did not know what he signed up for. He has been on rollercoasters before, but never experienced drops of this magnitude at this speed before in rapid succession. That is after the repeated spinning. After this epic ride ends, a dizzy Corey tries to keep up with Amaya, who then suddenly stops once they exit the ride area.

"Is everything okay, Amaya?" Corey said.

Amaya just bursts out laughing uncontrollably. This goes on for a while and then she finally speaks. "Corey, I have never laughed so much before in my life. Do you know how you sounded? I made sure to purchase the picture with that expression on your face. We have many more adventures to share together. Let's go," Amaya said.

Corey wants to redeem himself some other way, realizing that Amaya is in control of the situation.

The Black Hole is next. Corey and Amaya pair up together in a space capsule that is launched into a virtual space. They feel much vibrating and the squeezing of their capsule. Both instinctively draw closer to each other, holding on to each other for dear life. Then, they see the light and what comes out on the other side of the black hole reflects their answers to the questionnaire filled out right after the ride's entrance, while waiting in the line.

"Corey, I like this world. I enjoy what we do together," Amaya said.

"We are just getting started," Corey said.

After trying several more ride and entertainment experiences together, Corey and Amaya finally decide to get something to eat. There are no lines in the restaurants at Crescent Amusement Park. They are seated by their robotic hostess and given menus to order from.

"Corey, before we order our entrees, let's share an appetizer first," Amaya said.

"Okay, what should we get?" Corey said.

"I want us to share the spicy squid. It is one of my favorites. Is that okay?" Amaya said.

"It is okay," Corey said slowly. After Corey orders the appetizer, Amaya whispers something else to the robotic waiter.

Just a few minutes later, the spicy squid comes. Amaya starts smiling while she is chewing, in anticipation of something. Corey is silently saying a prayer to himself. The heat is on. At first bite, this exotic experience did not go well. The tears come pouring out of Corey's eyes and he uses his urgent water break as an excuse to eject the squid from his system. Shortly afterwards, a heart shaped supreme pizza is delivered to Corey. This is what Amaya requested earlier for Corey.

"Corey, you would do anything for me, wouldn't you?" Amaya said.

"I tried the spicy squid," Corey said.

"That is a start. What thoughts come to your mind from the pizza I ordered for you?" Amaya said.

"Since it is a supreme, you must want only the best for me. When you do something, you go all out wanting only the best results and to be the best. When it comes to girls, you are definitely the supreme version. You are the best," Corey said.

Amaya blushed. "Corey, you are making a comeback, but I have one of my own. You are my knight and I am your princess. Let's explore how we can be happily ever after," Amaya said.

Corey pours enough parmesan cheese to cover his entire pizza.

"Corey? Hello, Corey. This is the part where we exchange phone numbers, e-mail addresses, and other info," Amaya said.

"Yes," Corey said. Corey is definitely in a higher orbit.

After the two finished fine dining and even more delightful conversation, Amaya saw her family from a distance. She subtlety prompts Corey to go into the opposite direction, rushing him to catch a scheduled show that is further away. As they watch the show, Amaya wishes for her knight to rescue her from the dragons in pursuit of her. She is tired of the family's traditions holding her prisoner. She sees meeting Corey as fate and is determined to shift the scales in her favor.

Later, Corey participates in a short videogame contest and is successful in winning Amaya a prize.

"Are you sure you do not want something for yourself?" Amaya said.

"I already have my prize," Corey said. Amaya picked the doll of a brown skinned knight in white armor.

"Let us savor this moment Corey," Amaya said.

"Most definitely," Corey said.

Corey and Amaya continue on their way, not knowing they are being pursued by two men with black jackets, who visited the same gaming vendor after they left. Amaya then suggests that they take a lunar train to try to find their families, while really hoping that the train ride will take them further away from hers. While waiting on the bench near the train stop, the two men with black jackets came on both sides, preparing to make their move until an unforeseen event stops them.

"Corey, there you are!" Mr. Blakeley said.

"We were so worried about you!" Mrs. Blakeley said.

"Mom, Corey has a girlfriend!" Kisa said.

"This is Amaya," Corey said.

"It is nice to meet you, young lady. Are your parents nearby?" Mr. Blakeley said.

"No sir," Amaya said.

"Your parents must be worried about you, Amaya. We'll help you find them," Mrs. Blakeley said.

"That will not be necessary. Amaya come with us now," an older man said.

"Father, these are the Blakeleys," Amaya said.

"Let's go, Amaya," Mr. Watanabe said.

Amaya winks at Corey and walks away. The two families then go their separate ways. Amaya and Corey later text each other, vowing not to let their families' separate worlds destroy their world.

I AM A CARTOON

Enter Book World. On its menu is a collection of virtual reality games, where everyone who enters becomes a living cartoon character. If one wishes, the player can be the same cartoon character as his or her continual avatar for all of the games in this collection. Many more take on multiple cartoon identities throughout this collection. It is alarming that a significant portion of the population spend more time living as cartoon characters in a fantasy world rather than being themselves in the real world. Part of this is attributed to the real-world fan followers and monetary prizes one can quickly accrue within Book World. It is also astonishing how there is now a greater chance of making more money in Book World than the real world due to recent economic policies, which only benefit a small fraction of the population. The most coveted prize in Book World is obtaining the Golden Book. The contents of this prize are a mystery to be discussed at another time.

For those who are still unfamiliar with what Book World has to offer, follow along with a newcomer named Lester. He is a twelve-year old Afrikaner with red hair and green eyes, whose optimism hopes to overshadow his inexperience. There is a fire in his eyes waiting to blast off to the unknown. He has only known South Africa all of his life, and even then, has barely scratched the surface. He will soon experience what it is like to be someone else and the impact his new appearance will have on his journey.

Book World games are viewed and followed from television and computers, but are played from Book World centers, resorts and spas, and condos. Lester goes to the local Book World center. He puts on his virtual interface uniform and gaming visors and then walks through a virtual portal. On the other side of the portal is a virtual animated galaxy. Lester looks at himself in the mirror and sees a cartoon version of himself. Everything appears to be a hand drawn, cell-shaded cartoon brought to life. Lester is then asked a series of questions by a talking cloud.

Based on Lester's responses, he is struck by lightning from this cloud and is transformed into a chameleon humanoid clothed with a yellow t-shirt saying, "DANGER", with red letters, relaxed fit blue jeans, and high-top red, black, and green sneakers. The cloud gives Lester a new name, Gil. Gil looks at a mirror again. Much to his surprise, a long tongue extends out of his mouth, and his eyeballs literally pop out of his eyes. Then, the eyeballs come back in.

"Gil, hurry up! You have a lot of training today," an astounding ladybug humanoid said.

"What?" Gil said.

"Don't act like you don't know your girlfriend, Jewel. We are finally going to start our treasure hunting quest today, and I want my boyfriend to do well," Jewel said.

Then, something happens to alter Gil's mind and memories. He remembers Jewel, and a passion for her is programmed into him. "Let's go for it, Jewel," Gil said as he turns orange.

"That is more like it, Gil," Jewel said.

"Gil, this the beginner's part of the Show Zone. You will learn the basics here. This is a safe zone where no matter how much you mess up, you cannot die here," Jewel said.

"What happens if I die elsewhere?" Gil said.

"Unless you can find additional bonus lives, you have ten lives. Once you run out of lives, you cannot return to this universe until after three days. A lot can change by then. Let's not let that happen, okay?" Jewel said.

Gil tries to test out his new body, easily gripping the branches and jumping onto others. Gil reaches the top of the tree in no time.

"Not a bad start, Gil," Jewel said.

Gil gets cocky, leaping from a tree, confident he will stick onto the Hamburger Hut window. Much to his surprise, he does not stick to the window, falling to his demise below. Adding insult to injury, a group of flying pigeons release some excess material on him as well.

"Wake-up, Gil. What are you thinking? Chameleons do not stick to walls and surfaces. If you are not here, you will lose a life. Try to be more careful next time," Jewel said.

"Will do," Gil said as he turns green.

"I have your backpack. When we start going on our quest, do not forget this boomerang I made for you. Also, when you eat spicy things, you can temporarily spit fire breath. It may drain your energy, but you can mentally change colors, physically camouflage yourself, to provide invisibility for a limited amount of time. Do you have any questions?" Jewel said.

"Yes, when do we eat?" Gil said. Gil turns yellow as his stomach growls.

"Already? We can go to Sidney's Place," Jewel said.

"What about Hamburger Hut?" Gil said.

Jewel pauses. "It is true that your favorite foods are jalapeno cheeseburgers, fries, and flies, but people like us are not welcomed, there," Jewel said.

"Why?" Gil said as he turns blue.

"We are different. You are a chameleon and I have a dark face," Jewel said.

"That is stupid. Let's go there. Besides, we can't die here," Gil said as he turns red.

"Okay, but don't forget that I told you so," Jewel said.

When they walked inside Hamburger Hut, the place becomes silent. A pig humanoid came to the cash register stating, "May I help you?"

"Sure, we will take two jalapeno cheeseburgers, large cheddar fries, sushi flies, a deluxe garden salad, and two sodas," Gil said.

"That will be fifteen coins," the pig cashier said. Jewel interrupts and pays.

"It's on me," Jewel said.

"Thank you, Jewel," Gil said as he turns pink.

"It will be coming right up," the pig cashier said.

From everyone else in the Hamburger Hut, there was nothing but silence.

Gil is not used to this behavior. The people all around him and Jewel treat them with such coldness. People who stare frown at them while others turn their head. No one speaks and wants to be spoken to. Others at nearby tables get up when the couple finally picks a table. Is this what minorities experience throughout the world? Their food is finally served to them, even after several people who ordered much later than them. Even though the service is lousy and the atmosphere is filled with bias and hatred, the food is still quite good. Their pride will at least not allow that atrocity. Gil and Jewel enjoy their food, but eat it quickly to leave. Unfortunately, they do not leave quick enough.

A giant snake wearing a cape around his body and a miter on top of his head enters the Hamburger Hut with an entourage. A lower ranking member of his entourage, a cockroach humanoid asks the cashier to provide the usual. He quickly gets it. Jewel catches the giant snake's attention.

"You're going to be my new squeeze," the giant snake said.

"I am already taken," Jewel said.

"Nobody tells me, the honorable Kukulkan, no," Kukulkan said.

"You heard the lady. She's taken," Gil said as he turns red.

"Stay in your place. You are just a chameleon," Kukulkan said.

Gil spits fire breath at Kukulkan.

"Argh! Put it out you morons!" Kukulkan said.

The pig cashier uses the fire extinguisher on Kukulkan. "We are terribly sorry, sir," the pig cashier said.

As Gil and Jewel try to leave, Kukulkan's baser instincts take over and he wraps himself around Gil, squeezing the gray chameleon into a pulp.

"No!" Jewel said.

"I am taking you with me," Kukulkan said.

The Hamburger Hut came to life. The people were laughing about Gil's fate. Echoes of his kind not being welcomed there and needing to stay in their place permeated the atmosphere.

When Gil wakes up, he sees the pig cashier mopping the floor. "Are you the only one who works here?" Gil said as he appeared to be pale as white.

"Yep, I am. Everyone else working here is a robot. My robot cleaner is down right now. I also do not trust robots with money," the pig cashier said.

"Where's my girlfriend?" Gil said as he started to turn green.

"I am sorry to say Kukulkan and his gang took her. His mansion is right in the South Zone. The next ferry is coming soon. Here is a ferry pass. It is the least I can do. I don't mean you any harm, but your kind is not welcomed here. If you will just stay in your place, things like this will not happen," the pig cashier said.

"I am a citizen of this kingdom like you. I have a right to be treated fairly like anyone else," Gil said.

"That is true youngster, but things do not work that way," the pig cashier said.

"Why?" Gil said.

"That is just the way things are. When you go against that, you go against everything. Here, take a bag of food on the house from me," the pig cashier said.

"Thank you and maybe one day, you will understand," Gil said. The pig cashier snorted as Gil went his way.

Gil finally made his way to Kukulkan's mansion in the swamp. It actually looked old and abandoned. Gil started to wonder if he had the right address. Just out of curiosity, Gil rings the doorbell. The doormat reveals itself to be a trapdoor leading down to the basement, where he is greeted by a giant alligator who swallows him whole. Life one is lost.

Gil wakes up in the basement and sees the giant alligator again. This time, Gil quickly applies his camouflage and makes his way up to a set of stairs through a drain to avoid a pursuing alligator who still smells him.

Out of the drain, Gil emerges into a bath tub of a giant he cannot tell what this person is. The giant has three eyes and is singing something out of tune in dialogue unrecognizable. The dirt coming out of her body is alive and chases after Gil as he turns yellow. Gil climbs out of the bathtub in record time and slams the bathroom door shut as he turns white. Gil has never seen something so ugly in his life. Right after that, a giant bowling ball comes rolling down the stairs and smushes him. Gil's second life is gone.

When Gil wakes up, the cockroach gang has taken over the living room having one big party. Gil becomes camouflaged, still having to avoid the craziness of everything around him, all of the awkward dancing, the passing out, the swinging of knives, the broken glass, mouse traps, and other strange things. A yellow Gil makes it to the kitchen. Then, he turns white.

Gil does not have enough energy to use his camouflage. He is greeted by a crossed eyed octopus wearing a chef's hat with a butcher knife and another cooking utensil in each tentacle. "Good, the main course is here. The boss told me you were coming," the octopus chef said. Gil takes out his boomerang and when he throws it, the boomerang hits everything in the kitchen except the octopus chef, knocking down all of the pots and pans, the dishes, trays of food, and so much more. The octopus chef starts throwing his utensils at Gil. Gil manages to dodge everything while the loud party music from the living room grows more disruptive. The octopus chef leaps on top of Gil after he releases his boomerang one more time and misses. "I think I am going to eat you myself," the octopus chef said. When all seems lost, then the boomerang returns. The boomerang hits the octopus chef on the head when he tries to give Gil the squeeze.

Gil gets up and his senses are aroused by a sweet, spicy aroma drawing him in. The bell goes off and the mysterious soup emerges. Hunger once again gets the best of a yellow Gil. Gil grabs a spoon from the drawer and tries some of this mysterious soup. Gil takes one sip of this soup broth. Gil starts to gag and buck his eyes. His eyeballs turn one hundred eighty degrees within his eyes. Gil turns from red to orange to yellow to gray to purple to six colors at one time, and then turns black and passes out. Gil's third life is gone. A pair of rat humanoids later come into the kitchen and take Gil away.

When Gil wakes up, he is face to face with Kukulkan in his bedroom.

"Leave us," Kukulkan said to the rat duo.

Gil pulls out his boomerang immediately.

"Don't even think about. You want to see Jewel again, don't you?" Kukulkan said.

"Where is she?" Gil said.

"Let's play a game first," Kukulkan said.

"Why?" Gil said.

"You have no choice," Kukulkan said.

"I'm listening," Gil said.

"What is both a man's biggest strength and weakness?" Kukulkan said.

"His courage," Gil said.

"You're an idiot," Kukulkan said. He gives Gil the squeeze again. Gil's fourth life is gone.

When Gil wakes up in Kukulkan's bedroom again, Kukulkan is right there waiting for him.

"Do you wish to try again?" Kukulkan said.

Gil remembers why he came out here in the first place. "Love," Gil said.

"It is about time," Kukulkan said.

"Where is Jewel?" Gil said.

"Let us continue," Kukulkan said.

"What are the two things guaranteed to not be given to everyone but anyone can give it at all times?" Kukulkan said.

Gil thinks about what he went through earlier at the Hamburger Hut to motivate his response. "Justice and equality," Gil said.

"We are tied now. Winner takes all in the next round," Kukulkan said.

"Game on," Gil said as he turns purple.

"Which disease has a prescribed cure, but every time it is treated, it comes back with a vengeance, multiplying many times over? I will give you one more clue. What disease is so widespread that most of the people who have it do not even realize they have it?" Kukulkan said.

Gil pondered on this question, but the answer has been in front of him all this time. A reality check has emerged in this cartoon world. It is time he sings a new melody, admitting the truth.

"Your time is up," Kukulkan said.

"Racism," Gil said.

"Now, you understand the truth. You may now proceed," Kukulkan said.

Gil went through the door Kukulkan was previously blocking. It led right to a bathroom with no one in it.

"There is no one here! Where is Jewel?" Gil said.

"She got on my nerves and I let her go," Kukulkan said.

"What?" Gil said.

"Push the button on top of my toilet," Kukulkan said.

When Gil made it out of the mansion and started to traverse through the swamp, the first person to meet him was Jewel. "Jewel!" Gil said.

Jewel hugged him. "Gil, you should not have come here. I can take care of myself. When I discovered the secret passage and escaped, I later turned around thinking you will be crazy enough to come here looking for me. Now, let me reward you, my hero," Jewel said.

Gil's initial adventure wins him quite a bit of viewership and several followers. The body is but an instrument for the mind and spirit. The harmony of unity leads us down a true path to greatness. Love and truth are valuable guides.

HERSH AND NESSA

THE BIG BREAK

No matter how gifted someone is, it is not easy breaking into the music industry. There is more talent than opportunities. The volume of music releases exceeds the demand, while still not satisfying the unique appetites of many. Tours take over many performers' lives just to make a profit. Just to go through this ritual, much more is sacrificed. Sometimes, souls are sacrificed and spirits are bartered for other spirits. In those cases, who they know is more important than how they sound. The industry has a way of pushing music they like onto the masses, dictating what is liked and followed. Those who do not bow down to the shadowy cliques are shut out or shut up, whatever it takes to keep control. This philosophy has crept into many industries and institutions. In spite of all of this, many are willing to pay the price for an illusion of success and fleeting riches. Who will break the chain?

Being at the local coliseum brings a wave of excitement and spontaneous passion that are hard to extinguish. The crowd both loves and hates those charged with entertaining them. This is the time where stars are elevated and pretenders are buried. Even the gospel music business is not immune to the throes of the music industry. Two teenage siblings, Herschel and Vanessa, are going to learn some tough lessons about this industry and the difference between business and ministry.

Fourteen-year-old fraternal twins, Herschel and Vanessa, share a special bond with each other that is only matched by their mutual passion for music and singing. They hold hands together in prayer, claiming that this night is their night. It is their faith, talent, and determination that have gotten them this far. The top three music acts tonight move on to the national auditions concert for the Butter Bread Music Label.

The announcer, Sister Thang, came onto the stage to rising cheers. Her silver hat, shoes, and ear rings match her silver dress, which are contrasted by her golden blond hair and caramel brown skin. Surprisingly, her lip gloss and painted nails still remain conversative. "Let's all cheer for each of the singers, musicians, and choirs who poured out their souls this night. Now, it is time to announce who is moving on to represent us," Sister Thang said.

"This is our time, Vanessa," Herschel said.

"I receive that Herschel," Vanessa said.

"Now, the State Bronze Award goes to, The Wheat Gang," Sister Thang said.

"They got a couple of boos. How are they even up there?" Vanessa said.

"Still, a lot of people like their free-styling lyrics. No one booed us. Treat this as a good sign for us," Herschel said.

There are no boos when The Wheat Gang smoothly walks on stage, only cheers and much applause.

"Everyone, give a shout out to our State Silver Award winners, the sweet, soul stirring duo of Molasses Moses and Marvelous Miriam," Sister Thang said.

"They are really good, Herschel. Do you think the judges will really like us more than them?" Vanessa said.

"This is our night for a miracle," Herschel said.

"Tonight, we are witnessing a miracle when you consider everything these young people have gone through to get here. All of you cheered and wanted more. The judges heard you. Let's hear an encore presentation, of our State Gold Award winners, The Sunshine Choir," Sister Thang said.

The crowd went wild, but everything has gone silent, as far as Herschel and Vanessa are concerned. Herschel cannot face his sister who still tries to console him. The walk from backstage feels like a fruitless odyssey. Meeting them downhill, are their father and mother, Mr. and Mrs. Lancaster, who offer hugs and words of encouragement to a solemn Vanessa and a tearful Herschel.

During the drive home, their parents realize that Herschel and Vanessa do not want to talk about the state concert audition anymore. They want to focus the children in on what is coming next.

"Herschel and Vanessa, there are a lot of people on the East Side Nursing Home who need cheering up. Both of you are what the doctor prescribed. Will you be able to stop by after the prayer breakfast?" Mrs. Lancaster said.

"Maybe," Vanessa said.

"Mom, we have to network after the prayer breakfast. Vanessa and I are going to stay after we finish our song and talk to some of the local artists and pastors who will be there. Brandy has set up everything. She is going to pick us up and even take us to a meeting with Pastor Jackson from the Covenant Mega Church," Herschel said.

"I forgot about that. We will not be able cut out early on Brandy after all of the work she has put in. We're sorry, Mom and Dad," Vanessa said.

"That is okay, honey. We'll catch you the next time," Mr. Lancaster said.

The next morning, Mr. and Mrs. Lancaster leave to start their ministry commitment at the East Side Nursing Home. Herschel and Vanessa make it outside to wait for Brandy to pick them up. Time starts to go by, without them hearing or seeing anything from Brandy. Then, Herschel's cellphone rings.

"Hello," Herschel said.

"I am so sorry, Herschel," Brandy said.

"Brandy, is that you? You don't sound so good," Herschel said.

"I feel worse. I will not be able to pick you up today, but I have arranged Nimble Rider Services to pick you up and later help you meet up with Pastor Jackson and get home. Please give my apologies to Vanessa," Brandy said.

"Will do. I hope that you will feel better. Do not worry about us. Get some rest," Herschel said.

"Thank you. Bye," Brandy said.

"Bye Brandy," Herschel said.

"Is everything okay?" Vanessa said.

"Brandy's sick, but here comes our ride now," Herschel said.

A red car with Nimble Rider Services featured on its right front passenger door pulls up. "Hello. Are you the Lancasters? You have a prayer breakfast to go to, don't you?" the driver said.

"Who sent you?" Herschel said.

"Someone named Brandy. Let me show you my papers," the driver said.

"Alright, we're coming with you," Herschel said.

"Let's get going then," the driver said.

As they ride in the car, Vanessa whispers to Herschel the damage she notices on the back bumper. Something else starts to catch Herschel's attention sooner.

"Hey, we appear to be going the wrong way," Herschel said.

"Sit back and relax. I know a shortcut," the driver said.

Then, the car windows become tinted and the car rapidly increases in speed. Vanessa notices that she cannot unlock the doors.

"Let us out!" Vanessa said.

"I can't get a signal on my cellphone!" Herschel said.

"There are many great games we shall play, kiddos," the driver said.

The car keeps accelerating with the Lancaster children's pleas for help seemingly going unheard. The driver starts to sound more like a clown than a driver and keeps ranting about the games they will play together. Then, there is crash. Everything goes black.

Eventually, the car doors are forced open and the Lancaster children are greeted by the police.

"Are you kids, okay?" the police officer said. "What happened?" Herschel said.

"I have this killer headache that will not go away," Vanessa said.

"Let's get you kids checked out," the police officer said.

"What? We have to sing at a prayer breakfast at the Camelot Inn," Herschel said.

"You kids are not going anywhere other than getting checked out. Where are your parents?" the police officer said.

"At the East Side Nursing Home," Vanessa said.

"Depending upon the medical staff's evaluation, I will take you straight there afterwards," the police officer said.

"We have an appointment at the Covenant Mega Church after our singing engagement at the Camelot Inn," Herschel said. "You're a difficult one, aren't you?" the police officer said.

"What time is it?" Herschel said.

"It's time for you to get checked out," the police officer said.

The paramedics are amazed that both Herschel and Vanessa do not appear to have any bruises or anything requiring a visit to the emergency room. Even Vanessa's headache subsides. Both children are given contact information to make a follow-up appointment. Herschel and Vanessa overhear how the Nimble Rider Services driver responsible for picking them up is killed earlier and replaced by this child molester, who is fatally killed by an intoxicated pick-up truck driver that collides with the red car. The intoxicated pick-up truck driver also lives to tell the tale, but at least this story does not have a nightmarish ending for the Lancaster children. Not yet, anyway.

"Look at the time, Herschel! It is one o'clock. We missed the prayer breakfast and we are supposed to be at the Covenant Mega Church right now!" Vanessa said.

"Even worse, I finally have a signal again and Pastor Jackson texted me saying that because we were no-shows at the prayer breakfast, we are not reliable enough to sing at the Covenant Mega Church. He cancelled our appointment!" Herschel said.

They were knocked out from the crash, but not taken out. They are battered in soul, but not in body. The Lancaster children are happy in their spirits to be alive, but deflated in their souls about today's other turn of events concerning their music opportunities.

The police drop Herschel and Vanessa off at East Side Nursing Home. They tell their parents everything as they are embraced. Their parents persuaded them to share their testimony with the senior audience, which they did. The Lancaster children also gain new inspiration to sing a couple of songs to the seniors as well. This lifts not just the seniors' spirits, but theirs as well.

Later, Herschel and Vanessa hand out care packages to various seniors. They are then approached from behind by someone asking for a care package for his aunt. When Herschel and Vanessa turn around, they are shocked by who they see.

It is Jimmy Praise, one of the all-time traditional gospel greats! "Thank you, children," Jimmy Praise said.

"You're welcome, sir," the Lancaster children said.

"Both of you sung well today. My aunt, who stays here, really enjoyed you. You blessed me as well," Jimmy Praise said.

"We give God the glory," Herschel said.

"It is our pleasure," Vanessa said.

"What impressed me even more, are the two of you willing to serve and spend your Saturday with seniors. Too many of these gospel music artists have forgotten what ministry and serving are all about. All they care about is seeing what they can get. God led me here this day," Jimmy Praise said.

"We are glad that he did," Vanessa said.

"Young lady, I prayed to God to show me who to choose as my new apprentices. Are you and your brother interested, of course with your parents' permission?" Jimmy Praise said.

"Yes! Yes! Thank you so much!" Vanessa said.

"Yes, thank you!" Herschel said.

"Good. Let's talk with your parents and seal the deal. Today is your big break. Hallelujah!" Jimmy Praise said.

Some of our biggest moments come from the strangest or toughest of circumstances. Remain diligent, and realize that your gifts will make room for you. Your big break shall come. Just be ready.

Success has a price. Be wise with your decision.

TRIUNE HOPE

Another Sunday service at Saint Luke Church is about to end. Pastor Thomas is almost done with the sermon. Now, comes the altar call and then the benediction. It is what comes afterwards, the crowd anticipates even more so each week. After all of these years, Saint Luke Church is the center of its community once again. This church can afford to hand out cooked meals and soda to everyone who comes out each Sunday.

Three childhood friends, the twelve-year-olds, Brian, Amanda, and Chris, come to Saint Luke Church services every Sunday to be partakers of the feast that comes afterwards. Amanda does not realize that she is also an unwilling participant of Brian and Chris dueling for her affections and attention. Among other things, their friendship shall truly be tested this summer. The church building itself is quaint, but not flexible enough to accommodate the dining needs of the crowd that comes. So, everyone grabs to-go bags and soda cans. Brian, Amanda, and Chris grab their to-go bags and soda cans, leaving the sanctuary of Saint Luke Church behind.

Reality hits hard when they leave Saint Luke Church. Saint Luke Church is blessed to be one of the few buildings left standing, being safe, and remaining beautiful in this city. An apocalypse hit this place and the rest of this world, taking no prisoners. The survivors are fighters of their freedom, who sacrificed so much, the alien invaders no longer saw the Earth worth fighting for and simply left. The children will at least have a decent meal to enjoy before they have to head back to the slum ruins, they dwell in with bickering adults who are more destitute in spirit than their surroundings. The three children share their secrets among themselves for their survival and growth. Some of these secrets bring them hope and a sense of purpose.

In a dilapidated park, the three pre-teens eat their meal.

"Brian, do you still hear the other voices again?" Chris said.

"There is a voice that kept nagging me in the church service today," Brian said.

"Do you still hear the voice?" Amanda said.

"Aargh!" Brian said.

"I take that as a yes," Chris said.

"Brian, are you okay?" Amanda said.

"The voice is getting louder again and giving me a bad headache," Brian said.

"I have an aspirin I can give you Brian. What did this voice say? Do you know where we can find the source of that voice?" Amanda said.

"Thanks, Amanda. I heard Jerry's," Brian said.

"Jerry's is not too far from the park," Amanda said.

"Wait, remember our promise to each other? Once we start, we must be all in," Chris said.

They nod in agreement and then make their way to Jerry's. Jerry's Groceries is one of the last supermarkets remaining in the city.

"Where do we start, Brian?" Amanda said.

"On the way here, I was told to go to the freezer area. It is in the employees only area in the back of the store," Brian said.

"I got this one. I will take over from here," Chris said.

"Lead the way then, Chris," Amanda said.

"Certainly," Chris said.

"What do you have planned, Chris?" Brian said.

"Watch and see," Chris said.

As they walk to the back of the store, Brian and Amanda notice that all store employees are treating them with the utmost respect and doing whatever Chris says. A couple of store employees even escort them to the freezer area and leave them alone in privacy at Chris' request.

Brian and Amanda have to lead the search in the freezer area, with Chris in deep concentration. Brian's connection with the voice pinpoints the source's location and enables him to unlock the storage containment unit. Then, an alarm goes off. There is a short, liberated alien, who is very thin and frail, lacking facial features. Then, he speaks with a mouth opening from the empty face.

"Go to the zoo to help the others," the alien said. The alien spits out green mucus and then melts into a water puddle, which evaporates.

When store workers march into this area, nobody notices Brian, Amanda, and Chris, who do not say a word. After they casually walk out of Jerry's Groceries, Chris finally says something.

"I told you I got this one," Chris said.

"That was smooth, Chris," Amanda said.

"I must admit, you really are putting your time in," Brian said.

This is one of the secrets they share. Chris is gifted with the special ability to mentally create illusions. He gets carried away with his gift at times. He gets a kick out of being the pictured store manager on duty and making Amanda look like the president and Brian the vice-president of the larger corporate office. Brian is noticing that he can telepathically communicate with aliens and is starting to understand their language and technology. There is so much he does not understand about his gift. Amanda is gifted as well. She feels less than whole without her gift. She cannot wait to use it again.

The local zoo is a survivor. It shows the scars of war, but still offers sanctuary. The lack of funding for the artificial is compensated by the natural evolution of its habitats still being suitable for the animals. Many of the zoo employees live in the zoo as well. Both the employees and animals are fed well here. The zoo is showing its age, but still remains timeless. The zoo is now its own town with a toll. With a lack of city funding, the zoo is no longer free. There is a fee, but Chris uses his illusion gift to help them get in for free in this urgent circumstance.

While in the zoo, it is all silent for Brian. He hears no voices.

"How are we going to find the others with everything being silent?" Brian said.

"Hey, at least I got us in here," Chris said.

"And I will get us the home run. I got this one, guys. Follow me," Amanda said.

"Yes ma'am," Chris said.

"I am all ears," Brian said.

Amanda leads them right to the lion. She just stares at the lion and he stops what he is doing and comes to her.

"Yes? What do you want?" the lion said.

"You are the king here. Have you seen anything strange going on in your kingdom?" Amanda said.

"Where do I start?" the lion said.

"How about, have you seen any animals or people that don't look like anything you have seen before?" Amanda said.

"Well, you are definitely one. People don't talk to me like you do," The lion said.

"Let's try again. Is there any place in the zoo, none of your subjects know about? Is there a mysterious place, the others talk about?" Amanda said.

"Go to the giraffes. They are either onto something or on something," the lion said.

"Thank you," Amanda said.

If not for another illusion from Chris, people will wonder why a lion is starring at a girl for an extended period of time. Instead, people only see a lion standing afar and another girl just staring at him.

When they make their way to the giraffes, they are asleep. Amanda uses her telepathy with animals to wake up one of the giraffes.

"Who disturbs me?" the chosen giraffe said.

"Your king sent me," Amanda said.

"Oh, he did, huh? Stay right where you are," the chosen giraffe said. The giraffe gets on a platform in his area and stands on it, bending his long neck down to reach Amanda's head.

"I can bite your head off. What did he tell you?" the giraffe said.

"Your king told me that you know of a mysterious place that no one knows about. Strange people go in there," Amanda said.

The giraffe licks Amanda's hair. "You are sweeter than a lollipop my dear. It is about time someone believes me!" the chosen giraffe said.

"You're the giraffe," Amanda said.

"Go to the vet facility near the elephant's area. Now, I am going back to sleep," the giraffe said.

"Thank you. We're going," Amanda said.

The roaring of the elephants appears to be discouraging the gifted trio from further pursuing their quest.

"What is wrong friends?" Amanda said.

"Don't go in there! You will never come out!" one of the elephants said.

Amanda breaks communication, wondering if they are being monitored. "This is the place," Amanda said.

"I can probably hack into the security door," Brian said.

"I can help us go further once we are in," Chris said.

"Let's do this then," Brian said.

"When did you become the leader?" Chris said.

"Let's go guys," Amanda said.

As they started to approach the facility, someone grabbed Brian.

"Stop right there!" the mysterious voice said.

Everyone turns around to see an old male stranger in a trench coat and top hat.

"If you go in there, they will immediately spot you. What you have will not work in there. Let's leave here now," the old man with the trench coat said.

"Why should we go with you?" Chris said.

"Because we are out of time," Brian said.

Some men who did not look like zoo workers come rushing out of the veterinarian facility door. The elephants squirt water on them at Amanda's request. Chris masks their escape with another illusion.

The children reach the old man's van and they get in out of desperation to leave the zoo.

"Young men and young lady, you need to be more careful with your gifts. I have been watching you for quite some time. If I am watching you, maybe The Allegiance is watching you as well," the old man said.

"Who?" Brian said.

"I am Mike. We have a lot to talk about," Mike said.

"What do you want, Mike?" Amanda said.

"I have a mission for you," Mike said.

"Why should we get involved?" Chris said.

"You are already in over your head, kid," Mike said.

"Why us?" Brian said.

"The alien who died at the grocery store chose you. You want to do something about those voices in your head, don't you?" Mike said.

"Yes," Brian said.

"Now is the time to listen as we make it to the hospital," Mike said.

Mike tells them that not all of the aliens left Earth, even though the vast majority have. Before the aliens departed, they impregnated several of the Earth women. These children are seed children, who start to manifest special abilities around age twelve. Brian, Amanda, and Chris are likely seed children. A secret international organization simply known as The Allegiance monitors, manipulates, captures, and controls seed children. The Allegiance may already be monitoring them, if not already manipulating them.

Mike parks near the hospital. Mike gives Brian a unique object. "You will know what to do with it," Mike said.

Just by touching this foreign object, a revelation is triggered in Brian's mind. "Yes, I do," Brian said.

"Give it back when you make it out of there," Mike said.

"Will do," Brian said.

Mike looks at Chris. "Let's stick with the plan," Mike said.

"Why are you looking at me?" Chris said.

"Because you are Chris," Mike said.

Once they enter the hospital through a back entrance enabled by an id card Mike gives them, Brian activates the foreign object to set off an electromagnetic pulse blacking out the hospital and several blocks nearby. Not even the back-up generators are working. In the midst of this confusion, Chris has them appear as doctors with credentials to a special area. Brian has an authentic id card from Mike to open the necessary doors. Amanda communicates with the numerous cockroaches and rodents within the hospital to ambush the remaining security in their way. They eventually reach a special room with another faceless alien, but this one is a child. Brian hurries them, warning them that the electromagnetic pulse barrier will be ending soon. The alien child communicates with Brian about the secret way that is previously used to get him inside the hospital. The trio makes it out of the hospital, back to their rendezvous point in time. In their rush, they fail to notice the person in the shadows monitoring them. Mike takes the device back from Brian. Chris and Amanda are glowing with confidence, but Brian says very little. This hospital mission is too easy. What is the real objective of this mission? Are they already being monitored or manipulated?

Mike drives them and parks a few blocks before the parking lot of Jerry's Groceries. A woman familiar to Mike greets him and he lets her in on the front passenger side seat.

"So, these are the wonder kids. Wonder kids, you need to be more careful next time," the woman said.

"What do you mean?" Chris said.

"Lula just saved your identities by taking and giving me the only recorded footage of the three of you in this grocery store. You owe her thanks," Mike said.

"Thank you, Lula," the young trio said.

Then, the alien child comes to life, becoming quite animated. Lula starts to speak in an alien language and embraces her child. "Thank you," Lula said.

Mike takes everyone to an abandoned barn not far from the outskirts of the ravaged city. Inside the barn, the woman transforms into her true, faceless alien form. Both the mother and her child walk through the entrance to the silo connected to the barn. In the silo, they are beamed up to outer space to be reunited with other family members. Mike's van opens up and a car emerges. Before the young trio can ask their questions, Mike speaks. "Let's get out of here before the cannibals come," Mike said.

Seed germination has started.

CHILD OF LIGHT

REFLEX

At some point in time, justice will be served. Even if we do not live to see justice administered, there shall be equity of the matter before time itself ends. Some equity is paid in installments throughout multiple generations while other accounts are settled just with the primary offender. There are agents sent to tie up loose ends.

One such agent is Reflex. He will become an urban legend known for providing justice, when it is overlooked or forgotten. Reflex has no respect of persons. It is not known if Reflex is a robot, an alien, a spirit, or a combination of all three.

This multistory townhouse with a basement on Fiftieth Street is known as the House of Horrors. Many who enter here rarely leave. Those who come and go are facilitators of unleashing the horrors of this place upon the whole city. The experiments, transformations, and revelry that occur here can provide a lifetime supply of source material for any kind of restricted horror movie one can imagine. It is here, where an urban revival shall start.

All across the flooring, stairs, and couches are people laid out on drugs not knowing the difference between reality and fantasy, placing more hope in that which is not real than anything else. The music keeps playing, but by this point, everyone has lost their groove. Then, fresh meat enters the house.

A man wearing a black trench coat and top hat, covering his face with a facemask and shades, enters the House of Horrors. Some of the residents rise up to greet this fresh meat, begging for their next fix or money to do such. Many no longer even sound human. The stranger in the black trench coat initially appears to be unmoved. Then the entourage surrounds him to seemingly swallow him whole.

"Enough!" a man with gas mask said. He sprays something that soothes the demanding residents for a moment, allowing the stranger with the black trench coat to get through. "You're late. Get downstairs," the man with the gas mask said.

The stranger with the black trench coat just nods his head.

The walk downstairs is a descent into a dungeon serving as a gateway to Hell. People are playing with fire down here and even dancing around it. There is gambling and much profanity being exchanged here. There is no light other than the fire, which frowns upon anything good.

"Just because you are a district dealer now with that fancy trench coat does not mean you get to be late to meetings," a bald-headed man said.

The man with the black trench coat just starred at the bald-headed man not saying a word.

"What's up with you Andre?" the bald-headed man said.

Suddenly, there is a flash of light blinding everyone for a brief moment. In place of Andre, is a man with reflective and solid chrome skin. On his head is a solid chrome flattop for hair. He has both the bulk and the balance to be agile with this chromium skin. His is not clothed but that which needs to be hidden remains so. His eyes glow with light energy and his skin reflects the limited sources of light around him. The man with the chromium skin writes a message on the wall with light energy. The message states, "Andre, saw the light."

Everyone starts shooting at the man with the chromium skin, just for the bullets to bounce off him. This mysterious agent of judgment fires light energy from his hands, which leaves no one untouched. People are wailing, others are crying with remorse, some fall flat on their faces overwhelmed with the moment of touching the light, and others get sick, not having strength to move.

The bald-headed man is crawling while throwing up. With tears in his eyes, he asks, "What do you want, man?"

The man with the chromium skin writes another message on the wall with light energy. The message states, "Give me a name."

"Tiger. Who are you?" the bald-headed man said.

Another message is written on the wall with light energy. The message states, "Tell Tiger to meet Reflex at the Eastside Warehouse! Man up!"

Reflex makes his way back upstairs to provide a revival to those lost in darkness. He shares the light with all of them. There are various reactions just like before, but there is encouragement that some who encounter the light this night will change. The House of Horrors starts to empty itself out. Reflex leaves another message. The message states, "Reflex was here."

Reflex makes his way to the Eastside Warehouse and is buried by several crates. Reflex showcases his super strength, clearing a path for himself. Then, a whole host encamps against him. Much to their dismay, his speed and subsequent reflexes are beyond human. When he sees Tiger emerge from the shadows, Reflex shares the light with the crowd. It has varying effects, but no effect on Tiger.

"Who do you think you are? You think some new commando wannabe like you is going to change things around here? You're going down for the count!" Tiger said.

Reflex leaves another message. The message states, "Give me a name. Your wrestling days ended years ago. You can't stop me."

"Now!" Tiger said.

Someone fires a rocket launcher right through Reflex's back. Reflex has a big hole in his back and chest, and collapses.

"Let's throw this mess down the river," Tiger said.

Reflex's back and chest start to reform. Reflex rises and keeps walking.

"You're not human!" Tiger said.

Reflex says nothing. Tiger pulls out a flamethrower and unleashes this fiery blaze upon Reflex. This buys Tiger some time as he leaves the warehouse.

When Tiger reaches his van, he finds Reflex waiting for him. Reflex reaches out and yanks Tiger's special animal mask off his face. Reflex shares the light with Tiger once again, who bellows out a name, "Duncan".

Reflex takes what is left of the flamethrower and sets the warehouse on fire. His work at the warehouse is done. There is more to do elsewhere.

There is an area in the city called Purple Alley, where pimps and prostitutes reign supreme. Even the police who are assigned to this area, fall in line. One of them is Detective Duncan. He plans to prey upon a female who is barely a high schooler, until Reflex sheds some light on the matter.

"I have already made my deal. The light cannot reach me," Detective Duncan said.

Reflex rips Detective Duncan's driver's car door off and grabs him by the collar. Detective Duncan spits in his face as he presses the button of a device in his pocket. Reflex flexes two of his fingers inside Duncan's nostrils. Reflex hears the police back-up coming and flees. All the police will find is Detective Duncan's naked skeleton. Detective Duncan's characteristics, clothing, and skin are transferred to Reflex temporarily.

Reflex has one more appointment he must keep this night. In disguise as Detective Duncan, he easily makes his way through the Deputy Mayor's mansion security and is welcomed inside the mansion. The Deputy Mayor comes to greet him.

"Welcome, detective. Let us talk in my study," Deputy Mayor Franks said. The Reflex Duncan just nods his head.

Deputy Mayor Franks gently closes the door to his study. "What are you doing here? I told you to never come here! What are you thinking?" Deputy Mayor Franks said.

Once again, there is a flash of blinding light and the image of Detective Duncan is replaced with Reflex. Deputy Mayor Franks flees to the living room. Reflex just takes his time, but still catches up with the deputy mayor.

"Stay away from me!" Deputy Mayor Franks said.

Reflex leaves another message. The message states, "Your time is up. You have been recalled."

"No!" Deputy Mayor Franks said.

The deputy mayor's wife and son appear.

"Please don't kill my daddy!" the deputy mayor's son said.

Reflex uses the power of the light to reveal Deputy Mayor Franks' transgressions to his wife and son.

Then, the police and security come charging into the mansion, surrounding Reflex. The police and security mistake the deputy mayor's wife and son being upset over the presence of Reflex, when it is really the truth about Deputy Mayor Franks that sickens them deep down within their souls.

"Freeze!" one of the police officers said.

"Kill this terrorist before he charges again and blows himself up!" Deputy Mayor Franks said.

One of his security guards is ambitious enough to follow this questionable command and the bullets go right through Reflex, who is now in a ghost state. One of the bullets goes right through Deputy Mayor Franks' heart.

Reflex knows that when his density is in a ghost like state, his time is running short. He runs right through the crowd of police and security guards, without anyone being able to stop him. He takes to the sky in his ghost like state. Everyone excuses themselves to focus on saving the deputy mayor.

Reflex makes his way to an inner-city apartment, where a five-year-old boy named Abner is sleeping. Reflex stares at him with loving eyes like a father has for his son. When Abner wakes up, the ghost of Reflex disappears.

In the morning, Abner is greeted by his adopted family, including his mother, younger sister, older sister, and older brother. They tell him about the deputy mayor being in the hospital and his wife providing evidence of his connection with a drug cartel that is plaguing their neighborhood. Justice remembers and has no respect of persons.

THE ALPHA AND OMEGA CLUB

GANGS

A coalition of large American corporations financially bails the federal government out of its debts and subsequent deficits, resulting in these private corporations running the entire country behind the scenes. This leads to a domino effect of the state, county, and other local governments toppling over in their policies and procedures to fall in line with this privatized federal government's wishes. The governments at all levels no longer serve the needs or desires of the people. All that matters now is to do that which is most profitable for the sponsoring coalition of corporations. Some have whispered these coalition being codenamed Octopus Inc. Their hands are in everything. Democracy is nothing more than an illusion of its former self.

A twelve-year old African American male named Chase and his guardian grandparents are kicked out of their Georgia home due to new eminent domain laws and deceived into moving to an overhyped low rent condominium in Florida. The twelve-year old's older brother, who used to stop people from bullying him, elected to remain in Georgia, working in a factory to maintain his low rent apartment. This is a time when people work hard and own very little. Underpaid wage slavery and affordable slums are now the new American way of life. Healthcare is a privilege, not a right. Only those who are in favor with Octopus Inc. have a voice. Some voices will fight to be heard by any means necessary. How long can a house divided this much against itself continue to stand?

Chase's school bus drops him off a few blocks before Palm Condominiums, where his home is. Every afternoon he gets off the bus is a sprint some marathoners will find challenging. The only prize for this daily endurance is living to go through it again the next day. Will this be the day he loses out on the marathon for his life?

Chase is off to the races. The usual cast of characters are charging after him. Chase gambles on taking the long, detoured route due to past successes. This gamble does not pay off because more of his peers are placing their bets with the Scabs, joining them. They are waiting for him. Chase runs out in the street with the approaching cars separating him from his pursuers and barely not hitting him. Chase has to go straight through the direct route.

All appears to be clear until he reaches the last block. Then, everyone comes out, laughing at him.

"You had your chance to join us. We don't have time for scaredy cats like you. You disrespected us when you chickened out on us. Now, we are going to cut you open. Nobody backs out on us!" a Scab member said.

Terrell and Travis did almost convince him to join, but he remembers his promise to his grandparents. He promises them and himself to be successful in making a good, honest living. He cannot do this without school and a skill. Now, he is about to be schooled by the Scabs to such an extent that his life flashes before his eyes.

"Somebody, help me!" Chase said.

There is only silence from goodness when evil steps closer to slaughter him.

Then comes a mighty, roaring wind that sweeps the Scabs away, but Chase remains in place. Chase takes off like a bullet, but the wind repels him back like a magnet of the same pole.

"What now?" Chase said to himself.

"It appears that you have learned a lesson today, friend," a young male said. This young male appears to be similar in age to Chase. His eyeglasses shine brightly, complementing his crystal blond hair, white two-piece suit, and shoes. Accompanying him are two teenagers wearing hoodies, who say nothing. Their faces remain covered. "I am Simon. Word has gotten out on you Chase. The only capital more valuable than money these days are people," Simon said.

"Thank you for saving me from the Scabs. I have to get home now," Chase said.

"Wait, my friend. Did you learn your lesson?" Simon said.

"What lesson?" Chase said.

"You can't go it alone in this city," Simon said.

"What do you want?" Chase said.

"Let me give you a word of advice. If you do not join a gang, a secret society, or a club, you are pretty much done for around here," Simon said.

"Are you going to kill me if I do not join your gang?" Chase said.

"No, but someone else will. We are not a gang. Consider us an after-school club that excels in academics and looks out for each other," Simon said.

"What is the catch?" Chase said.

"Find out for yourself tonight at eight o'clock, Chase. You will be around scholars instead of losers, but no one bullies us around. What do you have to lose?" Simon said.

Chase takes Simon's card and they go their separate ways. The card says, "RISE ABOVE EVERY CHALLENGE. CALL BEFORE YOU LEAVE HOME AND ENTER THEREIN." Neither take notice that a third party is watching both of them.

Chase does not wish to trouble his grandparents, the Souths, with his school problems. They are barely making it financially with their combined pensions and social security funding. They are strong physically and sharp mentally. It is his desire for his stress to not become theirs and make them unhealthy. Chase also realizes that if he is killed, that will break his grandparents' hearts, potentially killing them. He needs protection from the gangs. Will he have to join a gang or some other group just to stay alive at school and make it back to and from home? Then, the doorbell rings.

"Chase, there is a nice young lady named Rudith, who wants to talk with you," Grandma South said.

"Coming," Chase said.

It is hard for Chase to believe that his classmate will visit him, especially one who resembles a princess from the Nile dressed in urban clothing. There she is, downstairs in the living room, with something to share with him.

"Hello, Chase," Rudith said.

"Hi," Chase said.

"Do you have a minute?" Rudith said.

"Sure," Chase said.

Grandpa and Grandma South exit the living room with Grandpa South winking at Chase.

"I know it is tough being the new kid in the neighborhood not knowing anyone. Are you being pressured to join a gang?" Rudith said.

"Yeah. The Scabs tried to kill me this afternoon for turning them down. Then, Simon and his crew came and bailed me out," Chase said.

"The Magi tried to recruit you?" Rudith said.

"Yeah. They are having an info meeting tonight," Chase said.

"Are you planning on going there?" Rudith said.

"I might not have a choice," Chase said.

"There is always a choice, Chase. There are alternatives," Rudith said.

"Are you trying to get me to join something too?" Chase said.

"Sort of," Rudith said.

"The Magi have real power. What does your group have?" Chase said.

"Faith," Rudith said.

"I am sorry, Rudith. Faith alone, does not seem to cut it based on what I am up against," Chase said.

"There is more, Chase. The Alpha and Omega Club will surprise you," Rudith said.

"I am nearing the end now, but if I survive, I can give one of your club meetings a try," Chase said.

"You really are going out tonight," Rudith said.

"I'm thinking about it," Chase said.

"Thank you for your time, Chase. Hopefully, we can talk again," Rudith said.

"We will," Chase said.

"Yes, we will," Rudith said.

Chase walked her out, with a gut feeling he is missing out on something more.

"Well, what did she say, Chase?" Grandpa South said.

"She invited me to bible study," Chase said.

"Say, what?" Grandpa South said.

"I am going out tonight," Chase said.

"Where?" Grandpa South said.

"I am going to church on Ninth Street," Chase said.

"How are you getting there?" Grandpa South said.

"One of the deacons is picking me up for church," Chase said.

"I know that girl means something to you, so I won't ruin it. You can go this time. Make sure you come back with some good news!" Grandpa South said.

"Will do," Chase said.

This is the first time in a long time, Chase lies to his grandpa. He is fully committed now. He calls Simon and a ride for tonight's Magi meeting is promised to him.

Chase is picked up by an older man calling himself, "Deacon". All along the way, Deacon reassures Chase, he is making the right decision and will be enlightened tonight. Chase is still feeling the rumblings of regret for lying to Grandpa South and not hearing Rudith out some more.

Ironically, Chase does arrive at a church, which serves as a front for the Magi. They enter the church's basement through a secret entrance connected to another building. Inside, Chase sees multiple people wearing hoodies or long robes. Many people's faces are covered, unrecognizable. The only light showing up in the basement are candles of various colors. Chase sees nine other seemingly normal young people similar in age to him. There is more anticipation than conversation.

"Glad you could make it my friend. We are about to start," Simon said.

"Thanks," Chase said.

One of the Magi comes forth transforming one of the peer candidate's shadows into a living monster that devours the other peer candidate's shadows other than Chase's. Their shadows are then replaced with new shadows corresponding with their new countenance. This Magi sorcerer nods for Simon to talk with Chase. Simon escorts Chase to the previous entrance.

"Chase, before the Magi even talk with new recruits, they give the Shadow Test. Everyone passed, but you. You are a marked man. You are chosen to be the bonus sacrifice," Simon said.

"What?" Chase said.

"I'm sorry I got you into this, man. It's my duty to give you a head start. If you can make it home alive tonight, you will not be sacrificed. Still after this, you better watch your back from now on," Simon said.

"This is crazy!" Chase said.

"Go now!" Simon said.

Once again, Chase is having to run for his life, with the odds seeming more impossible than what he faced earlier that afternoon. All Chase keeps hearing are various laughter and whispers, as the fog grows all around him everywhere. Chase keeps picking up the pace until he feels a baseball bat hit his behind like a homeroom derby. Chase then falls, since he can no longer flee.

"You forgot about us already?" a Scab member said.

In the midst of this great pain, a light bulb comes on with the crawling Chase.

"Don't you see?" Chase said.

"See this!" a female Scab member kicks Chase in the face.

"The Magi are sacrificing me to you so that they kill several of you in one easy spot," Chase said.

"The only one dying here is you!" another Scab member said.

Then comes that familiar mighty, roaring wind. The wind brings all of the Scabs together. Then, another wind pushes Chase forward, giving him a running start once again. In the fog, Chase cannot see what is behind him. All he hears are gunshots, screams, and the rumbling of thunder. Chase keeps on going, then someone trips him up again.

"Where do you think you're going?" a familiar voice said.

"Travis, is that you?" Chase said.

"Shut up!" Travis said.

Travis pulls out a knife, but before he can strike, a pair of bright high beam lights shine in their faces.

"Freeze!" an off-duty police officer said.

Travis quickly takes off, but Chase stands still.

Out of the regular vehicle, Rudith emerges. "Daddy, this is Chase, who we are looking for," Rudith said.

"Get in the car young man," Rudith's Father said.

"Yes," Chase said.

"What were you thinking, Chase?" Rudith's Father said.

"I wanted power to protect myself and my grandparents," Chase said.

"There is no power greater than the Holy Spirt, who comes from our Lord and Savior, Jesus Christ," Rudith said.

"I still have a hard time believing that," Chase said.

"That is who keeps me going in the police," Rudith's Father said.

"On tomorrow, both the Scabs and Magi will be after me. I can't go on like this," Chase said.

"Do your grandparents know about this?" Rudith's Father said.

"I don't want to worry them," Chase said.

"What did you tell them about going out tonight?" Rudith said.

Chase paused. "I messed up, Rudith. Can we keep tonight our secret?" Chase said.

"I can do that Chase, but how is that going to solve your problem?" Rudith said.

"You tell me," Chase said.

"Are you willing to hear me out about the Alpha and Omega Club?" Rudith said.

"I'm all ears," Chase said.

Rudith's Father smiled. "When we get to your grandparents' place, we will keep tonight our secret," Rudith's Father said.

"Thank you," Chase said.

"Chase, your days of being bullied are coming to an end. With the Alpha and Omega Club, you are never alone," Rudith said.

We cannot do it all by ourselves. We need God and each other. Just as it is essential for destiny and instincts to converge as one, we must come together as one people to overcome and conquer the greater challenges before us.

FIRST DAY OF SUMMER

Three years ago, an alien satellite places a barrier around the Earth, and whenever the barrier periodically opens, lasers come from the satellite shrinking buildings and other objects it touches, but vaporizing animals and people touched by the lasers. People are constantly on the run, living in motor homes and camps to avoid the lasers where predictions for contact are not always accurate. The lasers even change the atmosphere, leading to a viral outbreak, in which there is still no cure. Facial masks, social distancing, public gathering restrictions, viral outbreak fears, distance education, teleworking, and mobile living are part of the new normal.

Today, is the first day of summer for the Traveler family. The Traveler children, Travis and Nathan, are excited to finish another school year of online learning. Dennis Traveler, their father, owns a beverage distribution business, which he is improving in leading through his smartphone and laptop. His beautiful, brilliant wife and mother of their children is Alden Traveler, a professional cyber counselor, who greatly inspires her family and others. Dennis and Alden are true soulmates, in spite of their political differences of one being liberal and the other a conservative. They are more alike than different and where they differ completes them. They share their best with their children to overcome the worst around them.

The Travelers live in a mobile home they call the Traveler Mobile. The Traveler Mobile stops at Ted's Discount Membership Warehouse Gas Station for a fuel battery recharge and a gasoline refueling. Both the recharge and refueling processes are automated now to reduce opportunities for viral infection. It is now two years since hands-on refueling is considered illegal for safety reasons. All vehicles are redesigned or designed to have multiple fuel solutions with fossil fuels now being relegated as a secondary fuel source. All recharging and refueling transactions are purchased through membership cards and integrated currency cards being scanned. Dennis then drives the Traveler Mobile to the parking lot of the main warehouse department store.

Dennis and his youngest son, Nathan, leave the Traveler Mobile with their facemasks on. Alden moves into the driver's seat to be on standby. Dennis and Nathan go into the store and there is man fussing about the face mask requirement violating his freedom. This individual is promptly escorted out by security. Dennis shows his membership card and both he and Nathan go in. As usual, there are shortages on some items they are looking for. They make the most of what's there.

Right after they finish paying through the scanned integrated currency card, Dennis' cellphone goes off, and then this is followed by the store alarm. It is announced that an unplanned laser blast is now predicted to come this way in less than ten minutes. Everyone has less than two minutes to leave the store. Dennis and Nathan hold onto the accelerating automated shopping cart as they rush out the store.

Alden is waiting for them. Dennis and Nathan go into the back of the Traveler Mobile, which is the sanitization area, with the loaded cart. They will return this cart to another Ted's Discount Membership Warehouse. While Dennis, Nathan, the cart, and items are being sanitized, Alden drives off, finding an opening in the vehicle stampede charging all around them. This local Ted's Discount Membership Warehouse transforms into its transport mode and rolls away, just in time to avoid the laser blast. Dennis and the Traveler children witness the laser blast shrinking nearby stores. Alden keeps her eyes on the road.

The bank the Travelers previously went to near Frank's Family Fun Center is now among the shrunken buildings due to one of last week's laser blasts. The Traveler Mobile stops near this shrunken bank.

"Are you sure this is safe, Dad?" Travis said.

"It is okay Travis. Just hand me my gloves," Dennis said.

Dennis picks up the shrunken bank with his gloved hands and swipes his integrated currency card through the slot to pay his remaining bill pay balance for the month due to the bandwidth throttling and other internet constraints in this busy area.

"Now, let's head over and get some of the best hotdogs and fries ever at Frank's," Dennis said.

"Do not forget the spicy baked beans and western coleslaw as well," Alden said.

"Can we play some games as well?" Nathan said.

"Most definitely. We have the time," Dennis said.

"I know you are looking forward to the games Dennis," Alden said.

"Thanks Mom and Dad!" both kids said.

Frank's Family Fun Center is in compliance with the recent health and human safety standards to combat the ongoing virus. Outside of the isolated areas, everyone is required to wear facemasks. When the Travelers come inside with their facemasks on, they walk through a scanner determining their body temperatures, exposure to people testing positive for the virus through the online records database, and if any of the virus resides in their bodies.

"All clear," the computer scanner said.

A worker behind the glass window asks the Travelers if they are dining, playing games, or doing both. The Travelers indicated both and are pointed to an isolated dining area.

All dining booths are enclosed in isolation bubbles and automatically sanitized between each use. Customers' hands are cleaned through sanitizer dispensers at the tables. When the food is ready, it is served through an activated opening in the bubble. The clean-up process is automated as well. Gaming is now a communal, but socially distant experience. All games are in isolation bubbles with local networks connecting them for multi-player experiences. After a person exits the gaming isolation bubble, it is automatically sanitized. Multiplayer virtual reality games have replaced the play area type attractions of old to enable a safe, interactive experience with others.

Travis and Nathan enjoying themselves fill their parents with gladness. Their children are going through so much in the midst of this ongoing virus pandemic and heated racial pandemic occurring simultaneously. It has never been this hard in recent memory being an African American family. They try to do everything right, but still end up with mixed results because of what they are and others' perceptions of and responses to such. Alden notices that Dennis' demeanor is not the same since a text message from lunchtime.

"Dennis, you cannot fool me. Now that the children are playing, do you mind telling me what the text message is about?" Alden said.

"It is the same person pressuring me to sell my business to him again," Dennis said.

"When are we going to discuss this with the police?" Alden said.

"I don't trust them," Dennis said.

"Not all police are bad," Alden said.

"Neither are we," Dennis said.

Dennis starts to walk away, but Alden grabs his hand.

"I love you, Dennis. It will break my heart to have anything happen to you," Alden said.

"I will not break your heart, Alden. That is a promise you can take to any bank. Count on it," Dennis said.

Eventually, time does wind down and the Travelers finally leave to count down to other adventures this day. Travis and Nathan are still getting used to all prizes being virtual due to pandemic protections.

The Travelers ride in the Traveler Mobile to head to the Fair Land Campgrounds. There is a good mixture of nature, people, and supplies there. A virtual reality carnival is also there with real carnival food for sale. The Travelers enjoy this stop each year. Now, they just need to make it there.

While Dennis is driving the Traveler Mobile, Alden is finishing up a scheduled counseling appointment with one of her clients. Travis and Nathan are watching a streaming movie. Then, everyone's attention starts to shift towards the traffic jam appearing to go nowhere.

"Dennis, take the next exit," Alden said.

"We have not gone that way before," Dennis said.

"I know a shortcut," Alden said.

"Let's change places at the convenience store right after we take this exit," Alden said.

"I'll give it a try," Dennis said. Dennis starts to smile.

"What's on your mind?" Alden said.

"It sounds like you have a liberal solution in the works here," Dennis said.

"How do you know it wasn't your liberal solution that got us stuck in the traffic jam in the first place and I am finally getting us back on track?" Alden said.

Dennis chuckles from this.

So far, Alden's shortcut appears to be getting them back on track. Then, Dennis receives another troubling text message. The text message states, "You should have sold your business to me while you could. LASER BLASTS ARE COMING YOUR WAY!"

Dennis leans over to whisper to Alden. "Multiple laser blasts are coming our way. Drive as fast as you can and do not stop for any reason. Go now!" Dennis said.

Alden nods and the Traveler Mobile accelerates to what seems like a motor home grand pix.

"Mom, what is going on?" Travis said.

"Sit back and watch another movie. I am trying to catch a bridge," Alden said.

"Catch a bridge?" Travis said.

"When you get older, you will understand," Dennis said.

"Are we going to get blasted, Dad?" Nathan said.

"Not today," Dennis said.

Then, the flashing sirens come. The Traveler Mobile accelerates even more so.

They are now being followed by two police cars and then the laser blasts come, taking no sides. A laser blasts one police car, as the police officer escapes before the car shrinks. The other police officer turns around his car to help his comrade in arms. Now, it is just the lasers.

A laser just misses the passenger side of the Traveler Mobile. Alden keeps on going. Another laser just misses the back right tire. Alden then instinctively drives into the oncoming traffic lane. A tractor trailer soon appears getting ready to collide with the Traveler Mobile.

"Alden! We have to get out of this lane!" Dennis said.

"Not now!" Alden said.

A laser is strangely cutting through the lane they are supposed to be in.

The tractor trailer driver is blowing his horn. The tractor trailer tries to pull off, but does not appear to be in a position to fully get out of the way in time. The truck is blocking both the lane and the safety side line. Right before they collide with the tractor trailer, Alden makes a sharp turn to the right, diagonally turning into a rural post office parking lot, just missing the cutting laser, which changes direction and shrinks the tractor trailer. Then, the cutting laser disappears. Nathan notices that the running truck driver looks strange. He is then zapped by another laser and his scream is inhuman. Nathan breaks out crying with Travis trying to comfort him.

Alden gets them back on the road. She goes full force. Dennis checks his phone.

"Alden, another laser blast got the bridge!" Dennis said.

"I know somewhere else we can go. Hold on everyone," Alden said.

Alden makes a left and drives the Traveler Mobile through a tunnel leading to what is known as Haman's Hideaway.

"This is no Fair Land, but the chances of the laser blasts coming back to this area so soon are slim. We will just be here tonight and get back on the main road tomorrow morning," Alden said.

Haman's Hideaway lives up to its name of being a getaway in the woods. There is eternal shade with light shining through the covering sealing its approval of this habitat. The many animals freely roaming about catch Nathan's attention. The people are out fishing, jogging, and talking with each other. Travis and Nathan are puzzled why people are not wearing masks and there is no social distancing.

"I don't know about this place, Alden," Dennis said.

"We are Americans. We will be okay. Trust me," Alden said.

"I'll do this for you," Dennis said.

When they reach the campgrounds area, a chubby man without a facemask, blushes when he sees Alden.

"Can I help you ma'am?" the hideaway worker said.

"Hello. Are there any vacant camp spaces available for us?" Alden said.

"For you, there is. Go to Area 21. There is a station to pay. Enjoy your stay," the hideaway worker said.

"Thank you," Alden said.

Things are getting off to a better start here than Dennis envisions. Then, they exit the Traveler Mobile and it is a different world.

When the Travelers walk around in their facemasks, the people that are around stare at them. Wherever they go, others scatter like leaves blown away from an autumn wind. When some children come near Travis and Nathan, their parents aggressively guide them away, making no attempt to disguise their intentions. Alden can sense the irritation in Dennis and grabs him by the arm, focusing him on the old-fashioned general store. Travis grabs Nathan by the hand and they say not a word.

There is much chatter heard coming from the old-fashioned general store. When the Travelers enter, everything becomes dead silent.

"Can I help you?" a general store employee said.

"We are just looking around. Thank you," Alden said. Alden squeezes Dennis in the arm to discourage him from saying anything. Travis and Nathan are attracted to the classic candies that have become nearly impossible to find in the areas they usually dwell in. Alden starts to see an easing of tension in Dennis.

"You two just stole that candy!" an old woman said.

"No ma'am. That was not us," Travis said.

"You lying thief!" the old woman said. She hits Travis across the head with her purse.

"Leave my son alone now!" Dennis said.

"Your son is a thief!" the old woman said.

"Ma'am, is this man bothering you?" a general store employee said.

"Everyone, calm down! This is just a simple misunderstanding we can all work out," Alden said.

"Excuse me, there is a boy running out of the store with a handful of candy," Nathan said.

"Shut up, you thief!" the old woman said.

"You are not going to talk to my son this way! That boy my son described is probably the real thief," Dennis said.

By this time, the general store manager came in to intervene. "I want all of you to leave," the general store manager said.

"Let's go Dennis and children," Alden said.

"Okay," Dennis said.

When they left the general store, Nathan later looks back and notices the boy taking the candy earlier sharing some with the old woman.

When they get back to the Traveler's Mobile, and after they have all been sanitized, Dennis asks the boys to play a videogame while he and mommy talk in the kitchen.

"We are leaving this racist place right now," Dennis said.

"Check out this newsflash on my phone. The main road leading to Fair Land is now closed indefinitely due to an overturned tractor trailer and a burning vehicle," Alden said.

"We don't have to go to Fair Land. I rather be anywhere but here," Dennis said.

"A storm is setting in based on the latest weather update. The laser blasts really changed the atmosphere. We are going to have to stay put," Alden said.

"You are determined to have your way," Dennis said.

"Aren't you?" Alden said.

Then the rumbling of the thunder is heard and lightening makes her entrance known.

"We'll stay, but I'm getting my laser gun ready," Dennis said.

"People don't know us here. They will see that we are a good American family before we leave," Alden.

"If not, I am ready to share my nightmare with them," Dennis said.

"And I thought at one time, you wanted more gun control laws," Alden said.

At this moment, their passion for each other attracts more than repels, and they embrace each other.

The Travelers have a good dinner together inside the Traveler Mobile, and the children are comforted and further instructed on the laser blast zapping the truck driver and the bias treatment received in this place. Morale remains high and the children are off to bed. Even though the Travelers turn the lights off, Dennis and Alden see several candles lit on the outside with a crowd of people holding them. Dennis grabs his laser gun.

"I got this," Dennis said.

"No, there is a better way," Alden said.

"Hello. Can we help you with something?" Alden said.

"Leave this place!" one crowd member said.

"It is storming right now. We will gladly leave early tomorrow morning," Alden said.

"Your kind is not welcomed here!" another crowd member said.

"My kind? We are all Americans. We are all in this together," Alden said.

"Stay in your place!" another crowd member said.

"We apologize for any earlier misunderstanding. What will make you feel more comfortable that we only have the best of intentions like your average American citizen?" Alden said.

"Go back to Africa!" another crowd member said.

"I'm an American like you. I am even a registered conservative voter. I share the same good old-fashioned American values," Alden said.

"You think you are one of us?" another crowd member said.

Alden keeps talking with the crowd. Dennis is getting ready to use the laser gun. He does not see this conversation ending well. They are probably going to need to take off after a few well-placed laser shots, storm or not.

Then, Dennis receives another strange text. The text message states, "Since you are not selling your business, can I be a client?" Dennis texts a reply stating, "Sure, let's talk later."

Then a laser blast comes from the sky making contact with the crowd, zapping some and dispersing all. As Dennis gets ready to pull off and Alden runs to comfort the children who are starting to wake up, there is not another laser blast. The crowd is gone. It even stops raining.

"That was no random blast," Dennis said.

"Dennis!" Alden said.

Alden runs towards Dennis, bursting out in tears. Dennis hugs and consoles her.

"The American Dream is not dead, and neither are our dreams and our children's dreams. Love you," Dennis said.

GOOD FRIEND

Friendships can be found in all races and cultures. Take two twelve-year-old boys, the African American, Blake, and the White American, Tommy. They have been best friends since preschool and continually uphold a promise made in first grade to not let adults, politics, and society's ills divide them. They are so close to each other that the duo together is often nicknamed B.T.

Blake is at the community center gym puzzled. He is waiting a whole half hour for Tommy, when he has never been forced to wait thirty seconds for him before. Blake tries to call Tommy on his cellphone for the umpteenth time, and again, it goes right to voicemail. Blake eventually calls Tommy's mom, who is puzzled, because Tommy left earlier to make it on time. She does mention that Tommy did plan to stop at his favorite convenience store on the way to the community center.

There it is, the 6-2-12 Convenience Store. He and Tommy always loved this 6-2-12 since kindergarten. They have the best slushes and hotdogs and the latest comic books. Blake walks in and the store bell automatically rings, welcoming him in. Todd is on duty. Surely, he will know if Tommy stopped by.

"What's up Todd?" Blake said.

"Hey, B," Todd said.

"T and I were supposed to be going one on one again at the court today in the gym. He was a no-show," Blake said.

"What? T was in here earlier and he talked about schooling you again. Once he got his blue slush and cheese pretzels, he left out of here heading toward Smalls Road," Todd said.

"Thanks, Todd," Blake said.

"Good luck, B," Todd said. As Blake leaves, Todd pushes a button underneath the counter.

As Blake gets near Smalls Road, a pair of African American men with a dog appear.

"Sic him," one of the men said to his dog.

Blake ended up running down Smalls Road to elude the dog, as the two men laughed. While on the run, Blake trips up over a basketball, which he instantly recognizes is Tommy's. A bearded white man appears and hits Blake across the head with a baseball bat. As Blake zones out, he overhears the man saying, "This is the third kid we picked up today." Blake is taken inside a car.

Blake is later placed into a body bag and inside the car's trunk. The driver resumes travelling to his destination. When Blake regains consciousness, he continuously struggles in the body bag, trying to find some way to be free. It is too late. The car is at a complete stop, and the engine is turned off. The driver arrives at the new destination for Blake's bondage. Blake hears a couple of men talking.

"Our clients are going to arrive early. Help with those already unwrapped and frozen before unwrapping the others. The wrapped ones are not going anywhere," one of the strangers said.

Blake then hears loud screams and other strange conversations taking place. Then, Blake feels like he is being dragged out.

Blake is unwrapped and sees Tommy standing beside a man! Tommy signals for Blake to remain silent.

"We are going to get you kids and others out of here. The precinct is sending back-up," the undercover cop said.

Blake sees a few other undercover police officers. The same undercover police officer guides Blake, Tommy, and others out of a warehouse. The undercover police officer grabs Blake by the arm.

"Please take my cellphone," the undercover cop said.

"Sure. Thanks for saving us," Blake said.

"Just remember that there are still some good ones of us left. Now, run," the undercover police officer said.

Blake and Tommy run as far away from the old closed down meat packing plant as quickly as they can. Neither say a word to each other until they get back to Tommy's house. Even then, the words are few and far between. The two boys just sit in the living room saying nothing. Then, the cellphone of the undercover police officer beeps with the alert of a new text message.

Blake clicks the link with the text message and plays the video. Blake and Tommy witness the undercover police officers who rescued them being overwhelmed by a combination of the gang running the warehouse and mysterious tall thin men whose faces are covered. Whoever sent this video retreats to capture as much footage as possible. The police officer providing Blake the phone is not seen in the footage anywhere. The two boys hear a couple of police officers scream that the back-up never came and they were set up. Then, all of the police officers are literally frozen in motion except for the officer recording this video, who remains hidden. A portal opens up in the warehouse and volumes of frozen people are being transported through it. They also witness the captured police officers and other prisoners going through the inhuman process of becoming literally frozen. The mysterious tall thin men reveal themselves to be albino skinned bald headed aliens. They give their human trafficking partners a thumbs down. Each of the human traffickers then hemorrhage and die from induced strokes. The video ends with the fate of this police officer being uncertain. The odds are not in his favor, despite being one of the good ones. Blake and Tommy will never forget this day. These events will forever consume their lives.

Once again, greed and deception threaten to destroy mankind. There is one secret society funded by this alien faction, who hire various pawns to capture unwilling people to become slaves to these aliens. No one knows for sure how long this intergalactic human trafficking has been going on. The demand for human labor is greatly increasing, and there is pressure to greatly increase the supply by their alien sponsors.

These aliens are known as Genos. The Genos are a group of albino-skinned bald-headed mute aliens possessing telepathy with potential to also have telekinetic, pyro-kinetic, and other additional soulish abilities. There are both male and female Genos. They do not normally wear clothing but adorn themselves with painting their skin various colors and also adding different painted designs. The Genos possess plants and elements native to their planet that are in great demand throughout multiple galaxies. The Genos increase their profits multiple fold when utilizing slave labor on the fields and in the mines. They go to various planets, hiring natives to betray their own and capture them to be slaves for them. Then, the Genos conquer the native planet themselves, ultimately enslaving everyone when the planet is terraformed into a colony world. Slaves survive on the Genos' home world and on colony worlds by being transformed into pseudo Genos. The Genos have repeated this process for centuries, and now, it is Earth's turn. A day of reckoning is coming.

Wherever you are, please remember that greed destroys not just you, but others around you as well. Money works for you, but if you fall in love with her, you will become her slave. The liquid assets will become fire in your bosom that will curse you and future generations to come. Part of legacy is letting go of some of what you have so that others can grab onto new opportunities. Helping others rise makes all of us wiser and stronger. Do not let future generations become lost generations.

WHAT IS YOUR STORY?

Which story is your favorite one? Does mastering robotics give you a surge of enthusiasm? Do you instead have a drive to bring justice, in spite of the supernatural opposition in your way? What about acknowledging the truth concerning yourself and ascending to greatness? Do not forget the importance of being a team player to defeat a foe greater than yourself and a conspiracy beyond your imagination. How does it feel to be someone's champion, serving a greater purpose?

Do you know who and what you are, and the difference between the two? Who or what is inside of you? Do you understand the three realms and how they interact with each other? Did you know that a special calling requires special needs? What kind of balance do you need and how do others fit in that balance? Are you willing to overcome the sins and secrets of the past to change your future? You never know who you will meet at work. The greatest are right in telling you that the little things matter.

What are you willing to do and where will you go for change? What does it mean to have a soul and how much value do you place in yours? Love can come from the most unexpected situations and the strangest of places. What will you do for love? What does your heart tell you? How is understanding equality inseparable from addressing the challenges of reality? Do you have a special gift you love sharing with others? Knock on the right doors.

Which secrets can friends share with each other? Who is trustworthy? What will you do if you have the power to make things right, but only a short time to do it? Time is your biggest weakness which has no cure. Whatever you plan to do, there comes a time when you cannot do it alone. What makes a great team? What do name and family mean to you? How vulnerable are you to greed? How do you bounce back when you lose it all?

Everyone has a favorite. Please tell me yours. I have much more to share with you on your favorite story.

As great as it is to see, hear, reflect on, speak of, or read about someone else's story, there is no story greater than yours. God made it that way. He already declares who you are at the very beginning, before you are even born. There is no one like you and there never will be. Some are similar, but not the same. Not even a clone will do you justice.

Oftentimes, we come in on someone's climax or epilogue, not realizing that our very own prologue has set up the conclusion of things that matter most to us. Without having the insight of the prologue, we are at risk of living someone else's story other than our own. When we live someone else's story, we are at risk of not fulfilling our true destiny and handicapping our legacy.

Through understanding the premise of the prologue, you will be clued into how the plot comes together and your role in such. Knowing your role is derived from who you are. Who you are and what you are will be two different things, but must work together. One can dominate the plot, while the other is dictated by the plot. The one you decide to favor the most will determine your conclusion.

Whoever tries to dictate or dominate what you are surely does not have the insight to inform you of who you are. Neither does such an individual or group have the foresight to reveal where you are going. Be strong to not let the charismatic dilute your identity or detour your purpose. Remember, that you also have the choice to not let any clique sandwich you in between continual mediocrity and bondage. Your choices and words carry consequences and power. Rejection by those who do not know or appreciate who you are is no loss. You actually profit by not further engaging in toxic investments that never provide a justifiable rate of return.

You are your own currency. It is your job to prove how much your currency is worth in this exchange of life. The value of your currency is not determined by people's opinions, but by how well you respond to conflict. When you can be who you are in spite of everything else, your value will increase. The secret is that you overcome what others do to you by being who you are. Doing the exact same thing others do to you will guarantee a victory for your antagonist. Your antagonists' biggest weakness is always confusing what they are with who they are. The odds growing against you are only making your story more exciting. People and events can only stop or steal from what you are, but cannot defeat who you are. Even in the best of times, what you are is only temporary, but who you are is timeless. How valuable is your story?

As priceless as your story is, you will also be destined to play a pivotal role in someone else's story. What role will you play? Will you be a part of the conflict or the resolution? Ignoring such a role can eventually come back to haunt even the bravest of us. Fulfilling the wrong role can ultimately destroy us, making our ending worse than our beginning.

No matter how hard you try or how many times others have excluded you, no one is an island. You are connected to someone. There is someone who loves who you are. There is someone who appreciates who you are. There is someone who is dependent on who you are. There is someone who recognizes who you are. There are even those who hate or fear who you are. Make sure you understand why connections are formed.

Who are you? What is your story? Sometimes, part of your story is discovering who you are. Once you are awakened to who you are, you will never see yourself, events, and others the same way ever again. Others will know something is different about you. Some will love this and some will hate it.

Still, be true to who you are. Gifts and talents come from tapping into who you are. Who you are is that elusive "it" factor. Being who you are is the way to live a story that leads to happily ever after, having your ending become greater than your beginning. Greatness is not a fairytale. Just be who you are. Plug into the right source and a surge will eventually come. There is a purpose for everyone. This is a part of who you are. Go forth.

BONUS STORY

ENCORE PRESENTATION OF DISCIPLES BOOK ONE: NEW DAY

Thank you for your support of Vicenary: A Collection of Black and African Culture Science Fiction and Fantasy Stories. As one of my ways of expressing my gratitude for this milestone moment, please enjoy this encore presentation of Disciples Book One: New Day, which was originally published in 2018.

CLOSE CALL

"They are going to get you this time!" you say to yourself. You usually don't worry, but why else would they be at the school in your classroom? God's Enforcers (G.E.s) brought the law to several of your peers screaming throughout the halls. You don't know who is a disciple these days.

"Stay calm class. Just do what G.E. tells you when they come in," Mr. Winsom instructed. He's right. Some of the screams were accompanied by thumping footsteps silenced by the firing of electro shocks and lasers. "No one will be harmed unless you are a disciple."

"Kids, don't try to be adults or martyrs today," said an approaching G.E. officer. The thumping of your heart suddenly exceeds the surrounding footsteps. "One of you needs to be rehabilitated. Take him away!"

"No! There must be a mistake!" Mr. Winsom blurted. "Mr. Winsom!" the class shouted as two G.E. officers dragged him away. "Shut up and stay in your seats!" The shouting G.E. officer walks down your row. "Mr. Winsom has been harboring disciples for years," the G.E. officer said. He puts his hand on your shoulder. "Jerry Redmon come with us." Everyone is surprised to hear your real name.

You slam the textbook on your desk shut and it clicks. The light blinds everyone but you. You were trained for this. Mr. Winsom left the window open. That is how G.E. knew he was one of us.

After the light fades, you are already out of the window and running on the walls with your spider heels hidden in your tennis shoes. From the roof, no one is outside. G.E. only sent a small force against kids. Their arrogance is their undoing. Even in their weakness, no other disciple made it outside except for you. Hopefully, some found a hiding place.

You make it to the woods and take it one tree at a time. There are mines all over the ground. You can't depend entirely on your map. There used to be another disciple's house right after these woods. G.E. would probably search there next if not already. Stick with the plan. Trust no one but your family.

Stay off the roads. The yards near here are not fenced. Keep walking through the backyards and run if you have to. That time is now as a tailless black dog with a cut comes barking and chasing after you. Go! Go! Go!

"Hey!" You almost run into an older lady hanging up her clothes. The basket falls over and the dog runs into a sheet, later colliding into the clothesline pole. The woman runs inside. You have to hurry up!

There is a bicycle left in someone's yard. "No!" You must avoid stealing! You are a disciple! There is always a more excellent way! Time is about to run out!

Eventually, you see an old broken-down pick-up truck in someone's backyard. "Get under there now!" Just in time too. The G.E. force that invaded the middle school is going down the street satisfied with their recent spoils. You are just a kid. You could not have made it this far.

You may not make it much further if that snake slithering underneath the truck gets you. "Don't move!" The green snake slithers all around you and finally loses interest in you. The next thirty minutes feels like a day's shift as you pray and think about your next move.

It starts to rain. You definitely have a chance now. You will not be the only one running in the rain. You keep running and don't look back. You are homeward bound. Unfortunately, G.E. is already there. When it rains, it pours.

The good news is that no one's home. Hopefully, word reached them that your school was invaded. You got to get to the meeting place. The farm is not far. You will miss the church services in the barn. Who will be missed more? You or your family, if one of you don't make it there?

The rain picks up as you jet to the farm. Further turbulence is ahead. The corn fields you must crawl through take on a life of their own with the quickening winds. They make way to the rolling thunder stampede coming your way. Your heart beat still outpaces the stampede.

You almost nose dive into the muddy pool of a field from the flying debris and slapping corn fields. The emerging worms and cockroaches will not feast on you yet. No doubt about it. This is just disgusting. You got to accelerate.

The flashing light provides glimpses of death. Then there is darkness. Roll! The lightening on your trail just missed you. Not everything around you was as fortunate.

It's time to get up and take your chances. Death is haunting your either way. The frowning scarecrow tries to take you with him as he falls. Not today! Crashing into the barn doors still hurts, but you are able to walk away.

The doors into darkness have been opened. Something from the shadow emerges, wrapping its arm around your neck. "Freeze disciple! You won't get away this time!"

You feel an object pointed at your skull as the stranglehold tightens. You fall forward to the ground attempting to trip the stranger to the ground. He actually falls on top of you. Before you make another move, the lightning flashes a comforting revelation before you.

"Harvey, what are you doing?" you shouted. "What is your problem?"

"That is not your problem," Harvey said. He's right. "Argh!" "Jerry, just how many times are you going to get ants in your pants?"

"More times than you will beat me at spiderball!" you responded. "Don't rub it in if you want this!" Harvey said. "Okay! Okay!" Those blasted ants!

Harvey throws you a backpack. "You actually made it to the house?" you said. "Of course," Harvey said. Of course, the high school is right near the house. The change of clothes is a lifesaver! "Jerry, you're a mess!" Harvey said.

Later, you ask Harvey how he heard about the siege at the middle school. "Old man Grizzy told me as he was listening to something in the janitor's office," Harvey responded. "I guess you never know who is a disciple," you said. "Never count anyone out." "You're getting worried about the others?" you asked. "Yeah," Harvey sighed. The waiting game is never easy. It's downright suspenseful.

As the downpour declines, other survivors trickle in. Still, you don't see them. The growing number of candles and lanterns provide flickering glimpses of hope as you wait. "Hope that is seen is not hope: for what a man seeth, why doth he yet hope for? But if we hope for that we see not, then do we with patience wait for it." (From Romans 8:24-25, King James Version) The hope part you keep, but patience continues to dim. Where are they?

Weeping mothers are embraced learning of their children's demise. Tearful fathers latch onto their families with all their might. There is no guaranty they will see each other again pass today. This congregation knows that the local assembly will forever change after today's siege. Some have already departed; others never to return. There are the stubborn still determined to stay no matter what. The challenges of the future have already overshadowed the trials of the past. It is the triumphs that come at the end keeping hope alive. All present, make the most of their moment. Still, they are not here. What moment will you and Harvey have?

Farmer Bill calls the assembly together for prayer. Usually, those who don't make it in by the conclusion of the prayer either did not make it or already moved on. They would not move on without you and Harvey. Still, where are they? The prayer starts with Farmer Bill leading the prayer.

"Heavenly Father in Jesus name we thank you for life and the promise of life more abundantly you have given us. Please Lord, comfort those who lost loved ones this day. Spare those whose fates remain uncertain so that they can complete the work you ordained for them to do. Bless us to keep our joy in the midst of it all because you are with us. Your love for us is greater than any hatred working against us. Bless us to love others as you have loved us, never hating anyone. Deliver us from evil. Bring our loved ones home. We claim more survivors and victors. Lead us what to do as we rejoice in your name Jesus. Amen."

A rushing wind came through knocking the barn doors open. "People, a G.E. patrol is on their way here!" a familiar voice said.

"Dad!" you and Harvey blurted out. "Where's Cess?" you asked.

"Cecilia is already in the van. We have to go!" Dad said. "Harvey, you don't have to go. We can all hide in the chamber underneath till things cool off," Farmer Bill said to Dad. Dad's mind was made up. Everyone else was going to the underground chamber under the barn. We followed Dad to the van near the side of the barn. "Boys, this place has been compromised. May God help those who remain," Dad said. "Keep quiet and get down on the floor with Cecilia when you get in. People are still thinking I am making pizza deliveries in this van."

"Jerry!" Cecilia whispered from the depths of her gentle heart. You smiled and held your tearful sister's hand. "Cess, it is going to be alright," you said. "We are going to another sanctuary."

"Cess, it's good to see you too," Harvey said. "Oh, hi Harvey," Cess responded. "You're still upset about the salt squares in your tea this morning?" Harvey said. "I hope you get stuck with a spinach pizza!" Cecilia said. "Keep it down back there!" Dad said. Some things never change. Those are the things that keep us going sometimes.

No one said another word as we left town. You will miss Glotown, but Glotown will not miss you. Now that they know who you are, they will want to kill you. Here we go again is spoken again on the facial expressions of you and your siblings as you make eye contact.

Our prayers were answered. A thick fog emerged from the heavens. Many could not see, but we could. We could see that the van barely crossed the bridge before its scheduled opening. We believe the fog helped provide cover for Farmer Bill and other disciples. We do not believe in just the mundane. We have come to expect the supernatural. We live by miracles from a miracle. Many more are needed. Just believe.

DISCIPLES CHAPTER TWO

TEMPORARY SANCTUARY

We eventually got off the parkway and made a turn into the woods. This is not too far from a park you went to on a field trip. It is hard to believe that you were living in the same place for about four years. It is even harder to believe that a sanctuary may be near here. Still, if Dad drove any further, you would hit one of the cities where word has likely gotten out by now.

"Jerry, you took a risk getting up when you did," Dad said. "We're far along enough now where everybody can get up." Does Dad ever loosen up anymore?

"We might as well," Cecilia said. "Harvey keeps snoring." His snores are right at home with the crickets and frogs who welcome us. We keep going deeper and deeper into the silencing darkness.

The silence was short lived. Harvey's grumbling stomach finally wakes him up. "It must be pizza time," Harvey said. Harvey may be the thinnest of us, but he definitely eats the most. You will miss this van. It even has a power supply for the microwave. Cecilia makes sure to hook everyone up. Dad keeps driving while he eats. No one can blame him. Not even G.E. comes out in this kind of woods unless they have a big tip off. Hopefully, no one tipped them off to where we're going.

"Jerry, just how did you escape from G.E. when they came into the school?" Cecilia asked. "What did you do, Jerry, challenge them to a game of spiderball?" Harvey said. "Harvey, this is serious," Cecilia said. "Go ahead son," Dad said. "Basically, it was the bulb ball and spiderball shoes that saved me, along with Mr. Winsom's sacrifice," you said. "Mr. Winsom was a disciple?" Harvey said. "He was according to G.E. He left the window open for my escape."

"Was Mr. Winsom shot?" Dad asked. "I don't know what happened to him," you said. "G.E. carried him off and I just heard him screaming down the hallway."

"They will make an example out of him," Dad said. "They have a nerve to call themselves men shooting and beating up a bunch of seventh and eighth graders. Did you see anyone else make it out?" "I saw a few other survivors at the barn prayer meeting," you said. "You followed the instructed path?" Dad asked. "All the way," you said. "Good job Jerry," Dad said. "I am proud of you and so glad you're here."

"Yeah, how else can I get my spiderball rematch," Harvey said. "Do you only think of yourself, Harvey?" Cecilia said. "Jerry, are you hurt at all?" "I'm fine, Cess." "You were not fine with that mud suit you had on. You know I bailed you out."

"Harvey, did you go back to the house after you heard about what happened to Jerry's school?" Dad asked. "Umm..." Harvey said. "Harvey, you could have gotten yourself killed or arrested! You always go to the meeting place first. You should know better!"

"Things worked out," Harvey said. "This time," Cecilia said. "Harvey, the change in clothes was a lifesaver for me," you said. "Thanks."

Before you could finish, Harvey opened up the duffel bag he got from the house. He pulled out something that got Cecilia's attention. "Harvey, you saved my favorite doll!" Cecilia said. She grabbed both Harvey and the doll. "I don't want to lose either one of you," Cecilia said. "Please be careful next time. Thank you, Harvey." Tears started to slowly leak from her fragile eyes. As old and battered as that doll is, this remains one of Cecilia's greatest treasures. Mom gave it to her. Cecilia tries so hard to be like her. She always frustrates her-self with the same impossible task. We all miss Mom, especially Dad. "Harvey, I love you son," Dad said. Harvey's smile was priceless. "Dad, I…" Harvey said. Dad put on brakes hard.

We just missed the deer that came out of nowhere. You soon hear footsteps on top of the van. A wolf leaps off to pursue his prey. A confrontation is set for the final act of this drama. The deer puts up a fight, but darkness claims him like all the rest. The enforcer got his fresh meat. It is best for you to keep on going.

The lights go out and we enter a cave. "How can we see any-thing?" Cecilia said. "You don't have to," Dad said. "Just have faith." The van started to sink as you capsized into the underworld. The humming sound of a hidden elevator beneath escorts you further down your destiny. Hopefully, your journey will not end here. There's still nothing you can see. Moments like these definitely in-spire you to walk the straight and narrow.

Just as you hit rock bottom, part of the wall revolves and spins eve-ryone to the other side. Then, there is this blinding light promising judgment. "Retina scan complete," said an inhuman voice. "The Redmons are part of the Disciples Network. You may enter the sanc-tuary." We're home free, at least until a week. That is when a sanctuary council kicks us out to make room for others.

Everyone is now in a dimly lit parking garage. There are enough vehicles here to start a used car lot and maybe even a junk shop. Two men with red vests and laser guns come out to greet you. "Welcome to Sanctuary 56," one of the red vested men said. "Does anyone need emergency care?"

"The Lord kept us once again," Dad said. "Everyone is well." The red vested men embraced us as we got out of the van, happy that more brothers and sisters are still in the land of the living. "Brother Red-mon, we can fix up your van while you are here," the other red vested man said. "What can we get if we traded it in for cash?" Dad asked. "Brother Redmon, you will probably need to go to the Visitor Center to get more of the answers you are seeking." For Dad to not even con-sider modifying the van, where exactly are we going next?

We did not see any familiar faces at the Visitor Center. When we started looking at the directory map, we lost focused on Dad's goal. "Spiderball!" shouted both you and Harvey. "What about The Ex-change?" Dad asked. "Dad, I will go with you and help out. Please let Jerry and Harvey play. Jerry's been through so much lately," Cecilia said. "Okay, but just one session, and then meet back here." "Thank you, Dad!"

Spiderball is actually a simple game. Eight balls are launched at you the same time by the server and you need to hit back as many balls with your left and right-hand paddles as you can towards your opponent's court. The balls either one of you miss are caught by mov-ing web score nets and then served again. The game keeps on going until time runs out. Whoever has the highest score wins. The really fun part is wearing shoes and gloves that allow you to stick on walls and ceilings. For safety, everyone has to wear a helmet with a web mask.

"Jerry, are you ready?" Harvey said. "Yes, I'm ready to win," you said. "We'll see about that! I got first serve!" The robo server gets into position and is getting ready to launch eight balls based on the serving combo selected by Harvey. You have to get ready. Instinct must now replace thought. The robo server gives the green light. Go!

Left! Right! Up! Down! Climb! Jump! Right! Left! Missed! Back! Right! Left! Climb! Right! Right! Down! Up! Left! Left! Missed! Missed! Duck! Right! Right! Spin! Down! Up! Left! Right! Left! Right! Jump! Missed! Up! Left! Back! Climb! Right! Right! Down! Jump! Left! Right! Left! Left! Right! Right! Down! Missed! Right! Duck! Up! Down! Back! Back! Climb! Left! Left! Right! Right! Jump! Left! Right! Missed! Up! Duck! Left! Right! Criss-cross! Left! Missed! Jump! Up! Down! Spin! Left! Right! Left! Left! Over! It takes you both a while to get used to the slowdown of reality. "Game," you said. "You got lucky once again," said a disappointed

Harvey. "This is all about skill," you said. "Next time, the close call will go my way." Having confidence in another rematch reflects hope to be alive for another day. It is time to get back to Dad and Cecilia.

When you see Dad and Cecilia, you noticed a smile on his face and extra bags in Cecilia's hand. Dad must have gotten a good deal for the van at The Exchange. "We got something for you," Cecilia said. She opened up the bags and Harvey and I saw new spiderball shoes and gloves in our sizes. "Thank you, Dad, and Cess," we said. "You're welcome," they said. "Let's get to our room. We have to get an early start in the morning to pick up more supplies. This is a good sanctuary to stock up," Dad said.

Our room was not much, but it was clean. Carpet was too much of a luxury here. There were two sets of bunk beds with each set having a bunk bed above the other and one light bulb in between both bunk bed sets as the only light in the room other than the bathroom light. The bathroom only had an aging toilet and sink that was at least cleaner than what you will see at some gas stations. The tile on the floor did remind you of a gas station. The room had a neutral smell to it, nothing to make it feel like home or a prison. We miss our old home in Glotown already. You would not be surprised if Dad tries to rush the sanctuary council's decision on our next destination. After we had our family prayer, Harvey and I stayed up later testing out our new spiderball gear. "Do you think we will get assigned to a place like Glotown?" you asked Harvey while both of you climbed the wall near your bunk beds. "I hope not," Harvey said. "I am tired of the country." "You know how Dad hates cities after what happened to Mom," you whispered. "This council may not give us a choice," Harvey said. "Harvey, you may very well get your wish." We went no further with this conversation and turned off the one light in the room. You are nervous about moving back to the city again. The last time we were in a city, Mom was killed. Dad almost killed her murderer. All of us barely escaped being captured. Dad really cut it close and we almost became orphans. Harvey was not ready to lead us then. Who will lead us if that time does come?

With the way Dad has been purchasing supplies and gear the last couple of days, it is almost as if he believes he knows the way to Sanctuary 7. The first six sanctuaries were eventually found by the so called "gods" and their enforcers and most of the disciples in them were killed. Many sanctuaries have sprung up since that time, but Sanctuary 7 is supposed to be the only sanctuary that cannot be found and once you are there, you do not have to leave. You never have to worry about G.E. in this life and the next. One day after breakfast, Harvey goes off to a temporary job within Sanctuary 56 to earn some more money. As soon as Harvey leaves, Dad approaches Cecilia and you.

"There is something I must show you, Jerry and Cecilia," Dad said. "Follow me." We followed Dad to the sanctuary's library. One of the assistants escorted us to the storage area inferring that there was something we needed to pick up. Dad whispered for us to hold his hand and trust him. We walked in faith right through the wall.

The library outside looked like a yard sale collection placed on the shelves, but the small computer room we just found ourselves in looked like something from a spy network. Everything was 3-D and touchable. Holograms of all types and colors surrounded us, but nothing made a sound. A floating message also circled around us instructing, "DO NOT TALK! PUT ON THE EAR PIECES AND CHEW A PIECE OF GUM!" Afterwards, we could hear again.

A somber, bald headed man with glasses came up to us. "Do not ask questions," the bald-headed man said. "Follow me." We made it to another room and a 3-D holographic head appeared of a man with a beard and dark skin. "This is Philip," Dad said. "He came from Sanctuary 7 and provides carefully guarded clues to its location. The problem is that his clues are scattered and oftentimes encrypted. Even when deciphered, no one knows what he is talking about. It is not known if he ever made it back to Sanctuary 7 or is even alive. Still, pay attention." Dad told us about Philip after Mom died. This particular sanctuary must be the third clue Dad received. He told us about the other two clues He and Mom knew.

The Philip hologram started to speak. "Peace is not based on where you search for, but how you are found. When your heart is revealed, allow what is necessary to lead the way. Death may have to come before life. Your destiny will choose which comes first. Then, you will be in the right place. You must…" Then Philip abruptly faded away leaving behind a puzzled, sometimes frustrated audience. "May it be the Lord's will for you to understand this," the bald-headed man said. "We still have not found the way there yet." "Thank you, my brother," Dad said. "Let's go now kids." Dad did not want us to say a word about this to Harvey. Harvey talks too much. By the time Harvey got back from working, Cecilia and I were already in bed. Harvey mentioned to Dad that he was able to find work the next day as well.

When Harvey came back from work this time, everyone was up in the room. Dad wanted to tell everyone the sanctuary council's decision at the same time. We were all in suspense, even more so, due to Dad not eating all day and being of fewer words. After coming back from the council hearing, Dad had been sweating, praying, and moaning for hours. "Harvey, sit down," Dad said. "Harvey, Jerry, and Cecilia, this sanctuary's council has given us new identities and one-way transportation to live in the city of Allure. May the will of the Lord be done." No one said a word, but no one slept at the same time. Being sent to Allure is like a death sentence for a disciple. Will you even live to see your fourteenth birthday? Mom, you may be seeing me again soon.

DISCIPLES CHAPTER THREE

TAGGED

Before boarding the ship to Allure, we had to memorize our new identities. Even though in our hearts, we know we will always be a Redmon, for now, we must go by Johnson. You are now George Johnson. Dad goes by Ted Johnson. Harvey got stuck with Thomas Johnson. Cecilia fared better with a name somewhat to her liking, Chloe Johnson. Dad warned us that until our cover is blown, we are to use our new names at all times, both in public and private. Considering where we are going, how long will these names or we ourselves last?

The line to board Allure is always long. "Enter ye in at the strait gate: for wide is the gate, and broad is the way, that leadeth to destruction, and many there be which go in thereat:" (From Matthew 7:13, King James Version) The clouds gather as you progress through the end of the line and start to weep with what becomes heavy downpour. Now, your time comes.

"Bzzt...may I see your ticket and identification?" The floating droid asked. "Here you go," you said. The floating droid scans your ticket and id card. "All cleared. Enjoy your trip." The droid's slow, slurred voice was anything but clear. These cheap droids malfunction in the rain. The Disciples Network timed it perfectly. Hopefully, security at Allure will not uncover your false information. You run on board with the rest of your family. There is definitely something brewing.

Even inside, there is no escape from the storm. The horn sounds off and you sail off to face the winds of change. "We are going to make it there," Dad said. You wish he was equally confident about us surviving Allure. "Thomas, let's go to the mess hall and get some food right now. George and Chloe, stay in the room unless it starts to flood." Dad always plans ahead. He must be expecting this storm to get worse.

"George, do you think we should even unpack?" Chloe asked. "Chloe, this storm is going to be rough and we should only take things out when we must have them," you said. "It's going to be that bad?" "Yeah."

"Je-George, don't you just get tired of this sometimes?" Chloe said. Chloe places her head on your shoulder and you put your arm around her as you both sit on top of one of the small bunk beds. This small cabin does not have a couch or more than one chair. "Chloe, we will get through this like everything else, together," George said. "George, I love yo-oah!"

Already, the ship started to rock from side to side. "Chloe, hang on!" George said. Just then, a suitcase on the top bunk fell down. "That was close, George," Chloe said. The see saw continued and the only warning provided was through an intercom no one understood. The message sent by the roaring thunder was loud and clear, we are in for quite a storm.

"Chloe, let's grab what we can and be ready to head out when Dad returns," George said. "Okay," Chloe responded. We kept going from downhill to uphill as we gathered the few things we brought with us. Then, things went rapidly downhill. The lights went off. The lightning made its presence known, even at this lower level. The screaming overheard outside in the halls and other cabins did not make things better. Here come the looters!

As soon as we heard another woman scream, a rat jumped on Chloe's shoulder. "Eewwww!" Chloe said. You knock the rat off before he can bite Chloe. A loud thumping on the door puts the rat to flight. Chloe, must have alerted the looters! "Let us in!" someone said.

"George!" "Chloe"! That sounds like Dad! Is that Dad down the hall or in front of the door?

You pull a bat out of your backpack and hand Chloe a knife. The door knob turns. Then the door comes open. You swing your bat, but just manage to break a flash light belonging to one of your intruders. Chloe gets back. Then someone grabs the bat from you! Uh-Oh!

"George and Chloe, stop this now!" "Dad!" you and Chloe said. "Don't forget about me," Thomas said, as he slammed the door shut. "It's bad out there," Dad said. Thomas wrapped our sole chair around the door knob through the center hole. "Everyone, let's eat while we can." After we blessed our food and started eating, another loud thumping came at the door. The thumping got louder and louder. We became silent as our heart beats went into full gear. The invasion began.

"Ow!" a stranger said. Chloe had stabbed this man in the leg. Dad's shock glove took care of him and the other looter. Everyone was ready to go with luggage in hand. Then a pipe burst further down the hall released a vapor putting the other looters to flight. "Let's go!" We followed Dad's lead and went the other way.

"Come this way!" a crewman said with his flashlight. We made it to higher ground to see the lightning show. Just in time too, considering how the lower levels started to flood. "Thomas!" you yelled. Lightning just missed him. Everyone made it to the shelter and was given raincoats. In the air, you can see faces, none friendly. The worse is not over.

The storm takes us for quite a ride and we start to sink. Dad said nothing out loud the whole time. He just kept looking up whispering something. Then comes a whirlpool to bring about a grand finale, which none of us may be able to emerge from. Thomas tells everyone that he loves us as we go in circles. Dad says nothing. Chloe cries. Your frustration gets the best of you as you shout, "No!" to the storm.

Then something amazing happens. It literally feels like a large hand emerges from the river and places the ship in the palm of his hand. Everyone hangs on and we are taken through the eye of the storm and literally placed in a calm river. The rest of the trip is quiet, with few spoken words and even fewer questions answered. Allure awaits. Your paths will cross.

Then, that day finally came. "We're here!" Thomas said. For whatever reason, he always wanted to be in a city. He got his wish this time. We all wanted to take a look. We have been sheltered and napping for too long. No one had the best words to describe this place.

The water around the ship became red. The ship had to come to a dead stop as it approached a tall gate with two large statues, one on each side. There was a ship in front of us. The left statue has an eagle's head on a shapely woman's body while the right statue has a lion's head on a muscular man's body. The eagle head statue's eyes started to glow and blue lasers emerged from her eyes scanning the whole ship in front us. The lion head statue pulled out his right arm and then gave a thumb down with his right hand. The eagle head statue's eyes glowed once more, but this time emitting red lasers. These lasers set the ship on fire and piranhas emerged from the red river to devour those who tried to escape her judgment. We were next.

The eagle head statue scanned our ship as well but chirped something we did not understand. Then, the lion head status pulled out his right arm once again. This time, he gave a thumb up. The gate doors start to open and a light emerges to overshadow the darkness.

We hear a type of music throughout the atmosphere that is soothing yet requiring reverence. The waters here are dyed purple. We pass through statues of various sizes and degree of importance, shown through the gold, silver, and bronze selectively used. This was once the home of the man-made gods and their stench still remains here. A false hope is the only death sentence that people willingly enter. The hypocrisies of the haves and have nots are still marooned here. Justice is only as good as what you have to offer.

Allure is a metropolis with an expanding hunger for souls. Its numerous skyscrapers will put even the plans for the Tower of Babel to shame. There are numerous coliseums to appease the bloodthirsty, enough museums to poison the minds of the blinded intellectuals, an abundance of shops, restaurants, and casinos to make the rich poor, overbearing clubs and bars forever breeding new generations of alcoholics and short-lived entertainers, and unlimited venues to entice a lustful imagination. The population grows to keep up with Allure's deadly appetite.

In spite of the pageantry and the hype associated with it, Allure still shows the appearance of a fading beauty whose glory has departed. The man-made gods left for the moon and left this city as a memorial dedicated to their arrogance. A memorial is for recognition, not for true growth and lasting evolution. When the fantasy fades away, the lusts fail to provide the same level of satisfaction, and pride is humbled by something, someone greater, Allure will then have nothing left to offer.

The horn sounds off once again and we set anchor. No one is reluctant to leave the ship behind because of the intensity of the journey. The destination you have arrived to will present an even greater challenge. The stakes are higher and the temptations are greater.

G.E. officers are all over the place at the welcome center. You and the rest of the family are directed to one of the citizenship lines. An escalator takes you to a lower level. An unusually tall G.E. officer is behind you as you proceed through the double doors. The citizenship process is completely automated now. Still, you will now learn how prepared you are for this moment.

You are praying that the special eye drops everyone took at Sanctuary 56 have not worn off and will get you pass the retina scan.

Check! Success! Ow! A needle pricked your finger to make sure that your blood does not match the blood of any of the felons or disciples stored within the database. It is Dad who most concerns you, but he passes this test too. Of course, there is the irritating urine sample that is nothing more than a nuisance. Everyone's papers and id cards are scanned and thankfully checked out okay with the system. We are then forced to say, "The gods are with Allure and I am proud to become a citizen of Allure." We are then granted conditional citizenship to Allure and a G.E. officer tells you which subway train to go on. That same tall G.E. officer who walked behind you earlier now whispers something to the G.E. officer who pointed you to the right train. As you and your family walk closer to the direction of the train stop, that same tall G.E. officer continues to walk in your direction.

You and your family get on the train and you notice the same G.E. officer riding the train car directly behind, separated by a transparent emergency door. You want to say something to Dad or Thomas, but do not want to seem obvious either. This G.E. officer does not get off the train until you get off.

As you walk through your new neighborhood, which is a typical urban jungle failing to be as tamed as its distant uptown neighbors, you see the same G.E. officer walking from behind when you turn your head. You turn your head again and he is gone. Has your cover been blown already? Was the citizenship process too good to be true? Will you be arrested before you even see your new home? Have you been tagged?

Another problem emerges as soon as you reach your new home, which appears to be a high-rise apartment. There are numerous men and women hanging out, smoking and drinking outside near the apartment entrance. When they see you, they stop what they are doing. Before they, Dad, or anyone else makes a move, the mysterious G.E. officer reappears. "They are with me," the G.E. officer said. "If you or anyone else in this place ever harms or harasses this family, I will personally come back and purge whoever is responsible. Spread the word. Do you understand me?" Everyone outside nodded their heads.

Then, the G.E. officer looked in your direction. "Come follow me. I want to talk with you," the G.E. officer said. He led everyone to the basement area of the apartment. This is definitely a discrete location to shock someone. Usually, G.E. officers like to shock and arrest people in front of as large of an audience as possible.

"What do you want with us?" Dad asked. "Lower your voice," the G.E. officer said. "Let's not make it hard."

Dad said nothing else. For a short period of time, the two men just stared each other down. "Don't try to reach for anything in your pocket," the G.E. officer said. Dad paused. "Let's go inside this room." The G.E. officer had a device which unlocked the door without a key.

"We can talk now," the G.E. officer said. "For whatever reason, the monitoring equipment does not work well for basement areas in the buildings around here." Dad still said nothing.

"For the short time we have to talk, you must realize that I am on your side citizen. With the overflow in this apartment building, you were given one of the few apartments in the basement area. Where we are is your new home," the G.E. officer said. "How do you know this?" Dad asked. "I am a disciple too."

We were shocked. "I am Officer Albatross," Albatross said. "I see," Dad said. "I am your Disciple Network contact while you are in Allure. You can only talk freely in the basement areas of the old buildings. For everywhere else, you are closely monitored. Only pray silently in a resting position. For now, trust no one else here other than me. Within a month, I will introduce you to one of the disciple fellowship congregations, but still trust no one else for the next several months until I tell you otherwise. Don't forget to take "The Tour" soon or else they will become suspicious of you. Here is my pager number, but don't call me unless there is emergency. We will be in touch." Dad extends his hand and says, "Thank you Brother."

NEW DAY

We left in pairs in the morning. Chloe went with Dad and you left with Thomas. As you and Thomas get on the train, you noticed how lifeless everyone is in what is supposed to be a lively place. The daily grinds of life can take away from even the best and bring out the worst. As soon as everyone is seated, the train takes off like a roller-coaster. You have to admit, "You like this!"

The brakes that send you back to reality finally intersect with your stop. As you and Thomas get off the train and head up the escalator, you notice propaganda on the manmade gods all over the place. You don't get to read most of the propaganda due to having to concentrate on keeping up with Thomas throughout this heavy crowd. At least as soon as you leave the train station, you see your new school, Mary B. Ellis Middle School.

"All right George, give the guys a laugh and the girls your number," Thomas said. "Don't get played this time Thomas," you said. "I have learned this time. See ya". "Bye Thomas." A new day awaits.

"WELCOME TO GODHOOD," is the first message that you see from the banner hanging up as you enter the school doors. As a part of your welcome, you walk through a metal detector and your school id is scanned for entry. "Cleared," the God's Enforcer officer said. This school is full of God's Enforcer officers. In spite of their presence, a fight between two guys breaks out. Two God's Enforcer officers quickly come and slam both guys into the lockers. "Send them to Rehab," one of the God's Enforcer officers said. "Everyone get to your classes!"

As you rush to class, you accidentally bump into someone. "Excuse me, I am sorry," you said. "That is okay," She said. When you make eye contact, you notice a beauty unfamiliar to you. Her skin is dark and rich as someone from the African motherland. Her short black hair uncovers a hidden curiosity that quickly dominates your thoughts. Her clear nails display a perceived chastity. Her voice beckons you like a siren. "I'm George." She does not respond and keeps on going.

You make it into a crowded classroom which feels more like an auditorium. As you make your way down, it initially appears that everyone is too busy talking with their own clique to notice you. Then, a paper ball hits your head. As you turn around to find who threw the paper ball at you, you fail to notice the small laser ball used for school devices on the next step and it trips you just enough to fall. Well, Thomas is right. You did give the guys a laugh and as a bonus, the girls too. No one will probably want to give you their number though.

The chorus of laughter is broken up by the dimming of lights as you take a seat. This must be when the teacher comes in. The teacher suddenly appears, but not in a way that you expect.

"Greetings class," a three-dimensional hologram of an older man said. "Welcome George Johnson." You pause. "Are you okay from your fall?" the holographic teacher asked. "Yes," you said. "Let it be known that we are watching you and the gods see you all. Who among you will make history or be history? Let us continue on with our history lecture."

This history class is nothing like the ones you have experienced before. The rural towns you came from always taught the history of how things were before the birth of the gods. Right in the lesson's introduction, the class is told to disregard the B.C. and A.D. timelines. The harsh words spoken were, "Jesus Christ is dead and He is not coming back for His deluded followers that remain attached to such a fantasy. This is why we have the gods, to bring reality to divinity and hope. We no longer have to hope for better days, we can make new millenniums ourselves. While you are in Allure, you shall focus on the A.G. timeline, the arrival of the gods. Nothing else really matters before then." You have to put up with this propaganda for a full ninety minutes. This lesson primarily focused on some of the history of Allure, the good old days before the gods abandoned it like a politician drops a harlot when morning arrives. Allure has definitely seen better times. Her present state is a father's worst nightmare of his daughter.

At least the math class is smaller. Unfortunately, there is no real teacher. The holographic image is multiple pre-recordings of people partnered with artificial intelligence. Everyone follows along on interactive tablets. The computer instructor follows your personal progress on the tablet and the screen points out learning tips tailored for you. Math ends with the computer instructor telling everyone, "Those who do not know math and science are prisoners of imagination instead of being gods in reality," You then must click that you completed the lesson and sign off. "You can only have faith in what you know." Those final words are truer than it thinks. You know the truth and it shall make you free.

Finally, lunchtime is here. Dad always has you buy lunch because he usually just does not have the time to pack everyone a lunch. You really miss mom's lunches and her even more so. At least buying lunch will decrease the amount of time you will have to sit around the cafeteria. The food is far from alluring. The mystery meat accompanied by raw seasoned vegetables and dry fruit will have to do. Now comes the hard part.

As you make your way to the tables, some frown while others turn their heads. The seats quickly fill up when you are around and additional people are quick to shake their heads and tell you empty seats are reserved for people, who you suspect will likely never come. You finally see a table with empty chairs ahead of you with only two people at the table. One of the faces is actually familiar, the girl of your dreams that you encountered earlier is there! You quickly make your way over there, ignoring the strange person who is also sitting there.

As soon as you get to the table, she leaves without saying anything to you. You are left sitting near a guy with a robot suit on. "Who are you?" the guy in the robot suit said. "George," you said. He then says nothing. Who is this guy? "You have my name. What's yours?"

"Trevor," the guy in the robot suit said. "It is good to meet you Trevor," you said. "George, have you been on the tour yet?" "No."

"When I went on the tour, the werewolves did this to me and I have to wear this monkey suit just to keep breathing," Trevor said. "Werewolves?" you said. "If you don't want to believe me, you better believe this, stay away from Kim!" "Kim, who?" you replied.

"I know you want Kim Guardia, but she's mine," Trevor said. "I do not see a ring on her finger or yours," you said. "Do not try me George." You walk away before this gets nastier than the food you have leftover.

You are so upset that you fail to notice the milk carton on the floor and trip over it as your tray flies sideways slamming into Trevor's face. He throws some of your old leftovers back at your face and shouts something about your mother. Both of you got everyone's attention in the cafeteria. The fight is on! How do you fight a guy in a robot suit?

For emergency escapes, Dad did give you a set of little dissolving plastic balls with a sensor in it that will trigger most ceiling fire extinguishers. You reach into your pocket to seemingly pull out a mechanical pencil but activate the sensor. Before Trevor can punch you, all of the cafeteria fire extinguishers go off showering everyone with water and foam. As people take flight, the fight is interrupted. As you reach the door, a God's Enforcer officer is there to greet you. "Get down on your knees now," the God's Enforcer officer said. You comply to not get shocked. "You are coming to Rehab with me now!" As you walk, you notice Trevor being carried away and a long wire from his back exposed with foam. You hear whispers of him being trampled and you are in trouble.

You are escorted to a quiet hallway leading down to a dimly lit staircase taking you to a basement area. A metal door opens and your ears are opened to the horrors others are experiencing. Before you can respond, a blindfold is placed around your eyes and you are thrown down a chute where you feel a heater drying you off as you slide down into a couch. You also felt several robotic hands inspecting you and scanning you along the way. Your blindfold is also removed.

A pale skinned man with a bald head is there waiting for you. "George, you are new here," the pale skinned man said. "Yes," you said. "Let me educate you quickly, young man. We have the highest of standards in Allure and you are going to use your free period to think about them. Do not worry. You will make your biology class on time. This amoeba droid will get you up to speed quickly"

This disgusting tiny liquid robot is forced into your left nostril and you black out, awakening to another world going in hyper speed. You see several teenagers turning into werewolves and shot down while hearing a voice saying, "You become a monster when you reject the gods and the gods will kill you." Then, some magicians appear and they are stepped on like insects by a god's big foot while hearing a voice saying, "There is no power greater than the gods. Obey! Obey!" You then see several men and women transform from weak, depressed people to super beings full of joy and strength while hearing a voice saying, "If you obey, you will be rewarded with longer mortality or even immortality itself. Obey! Obey!" The same messages keep repeating themselves with different images becoming more surreal and fast forwarding at different speeds. You head feels like it is exploding as the amoeba droid dissolves. You are left a screaming mess and then wake up right at the entrance of your biology class.

Various people stare at you but say nothing to you. You are too spaced out to notice that Kim Guardia is sitting right behind you, leaving a note on your desk. This is the first class where you see a teacher in person. The whole class is a slide show featuring clips on how various animals were transformed when the god experiments were conducted on them before humans. You will be dissecting clones of some of the mutated animals throughout the year. Is this teacher really human? All of this is intended to show you the greatness of the manmade gods.

This school day is over and Thomas is leaning over right of the school entrance barely able to stand. "Ready, George?" Thomas asked. "Yes, but are you okay Thomas?" "Food poisoning from the mystery meat." Thomas said. You help Thomas get to the train, praying that he will not throw up along the way. Your headache keeps you distracted. This is one of those days.

As soon as you get home, Thomas runs into the bathroom and vomits out a big one, followed by a series of diarrhea. Count your blessings that this apartment does have a second half bathroom. Then you collapse.

You wake up and you see Dad, Chloe, and Thomas. "George, what happened?" Dad asked. You give him a recap of everything that happened except using one of the plastic sensor balls and what happened during free period. Unfortunately, you do not even remember what happened during free period. Of course, Dad admonishes you to not continue fighting and avoiding trouble at all costs. He also tells you, "Emergency protocols are not to be used for personal fights," Dad said. "Sorry, Dad," you said. He knew that you used a plastic ball. "George, I am just happy that you are okay. I do not want you to end up at Sister Southern's Hospital where I work at. It is not somewhere you want to be, even if you work there." Dad does not like his new job. "George, I made friends with several girls today at school who love wearing dresses like me," Chloe said. "Chloe, I am glad that your first day turned out better than mine," you said. "George, do you think they are disciples?" "Remember, where we are Chloe." Chloe smiles in response.

Thomas does not bother to talk about his school day, but you later hear him talking to someone over the phone in the bedroom with the door closed. This reminds you about a note you got from Kim Guardia you somehow forgot about. What really happened at school? You open the note and it reads, "Thank you. Give me your number. We will talk later." This is truly a new day with new opportunities. You sleep well with your thoughts being refocused.

GET MORE INSPIRATION FROM
APOSTOLIC PENTECOSTAL ALLIANCE BOOKS LLC!
www.apabooksllc.com

30-Day Bible Study Book

30-Day Bible Study Book is intended to help people learn how to use the Bible to make their lives better. Sometimes, the practical applications of the Bible are overlooked or not known. 30-Day Bible Study Book bridges the gap, containing thirty accessible bible study lessons that will provide revelation, inspiration, and transformation and help address several of the key issues of life. Some of the topics include understanding how to use the Bible, scriptural interpretation, salvation, deliverance, prayer, healing, finances, spiritual authority, spiritual gifts, purpose, finding a soulmate, marriage, stress management, success, end times, dispensations, covenants, ages, witnessing, discipleship, and more. This bible study book is ideal for personal growth and devotions, church bible studies, small group bible studies, and those studying the applicability of the New Testament in their lives. Notes pages are also included with each lesson.
Check out: https://store.bookbaby.com/book/30-day-bible-study-book

Happiness as an Independent Variable Second Edition

Wouldn't you rather be happy instead of sad, angry, or worried? Our traditional perceptions and common understandings of happiness oftentimes fail to lead us to true happiness. With this book, you will discover that happiness must be treated as an independent variable if you are to have and maintain the long-term state of happiness. This is available in printed and e-book editions. Discover more at: https://store.bookbaby.com/book/happiness-as-an-independent-variable

GEORGE ALLEN BLACKEN

Elder George Allen Blacken is the pastor of Holy Temple Cross Ministries Inc. in the Akron, Ohio area, where the primary focus is helping everyone obtain spiritual and natural successes. Elder Blacken was ordained by Bible Way World Wide in 2009 after graduating from the Bible Way Bible College. He previously graduated Summa Cum Laude at Florida A&M University and Old Dominion University for his undergraduate and graduate engineering degrees. He has written Happiness as an Independent Variable, Using the Power Within, 30-Day Bible Study Book, Disciples Book One: New Day, and Vicenary: A Collection of Black and African Culture Science Fiction and Fantasy Stories.

IF YOU LOVE VICENARY, PLEASE PROVIDE A REVIEW ON AMAZON AT:

https://www.amazon.com/review/create-review/?ie=UTF8&channel=glance-detail&asin=B08NVF1PCV

Made in the USA
Middletown, DE
16 March 2022

62624526R00116